D0997432

A Creepy Company

By the same author:

A BUNDLE OF NERVES

A TOUCH OF CHILL

A WHISPER IN THE NIGHT

A GOOSE ON YOUR GRAVE

A FIT OF SHIVERS

A Creepy Company

Joan Aiken

VICTOR GOLLANCZ
LONDON

First published in Great Britain 1993
by Victor Gollancz
an imprint of Cassell
Villiers House, 41/47 Strand, London WC2N 5JE

A catalogue record for this book is available from the British Library

ISBN 0 575 05544 8

Photoset in Great Britain by
Rowland Phototypesetting Ltd, Bury St Edmunds, Suffolk
and printed by St Edmundsbury Press Ltd,
Bury St Edmunds, Suffolk

Contents

To Richard Dalby

Dead Man's Lane

If you run hot water over the top of the whistling kettle, it lets out a howl, did you know that? I always do it when I go to my father's house, he has a whistler, and young Andy, my half-brother, he's only five, he always says, "*Don't*, Sam! Don't *do* that! You're hurting it!" Which makes me laugh.

Matter of fact, I don't go to my father's house a lot. We haven't much to say to each other. He moved last year—with my stepmother and the twins—out to this small country town, Crowbridge. It's an hour on the bike to get there. It's true he gave me the bike so that I could. And now he's promised to take me to Paris for a week, but only if I pass my exams. Which are coming up in a couple of weeks. So . . .

No problem about the exams, mind you. None that I can see. I don't know why Dad gets into such a fuss. He wrote me a letter saying he'd heard from the Old Swine that I wasn't doing as well in class as I should. Should! Who the hell is going to lay down the law about how well I should do?

Anyway, I'll be perfectly OK. Apart from anything else, I know this guy who can sell you a pen that guarantees you pass. And as well as the pen—which costs a fair slice, I will admit, but I'm going to ask Dad for an advance on my summer quarter's allowance—as well as the pen, the guy has this stuff. And the stuff is truly, truly five-dimensional. Gives you a lift right out of your own mind into something a hundred per cent higher and faster. The Great Chief Mind, maybe.

So—like I say—I don't go to Dad's place all that often any more.

When I do go, Ann, that's my stepmother, always gives me a great big hello, welcome on the mat, all that, but I reckon it can't be very sincere. Why should she be pleased to see me, anyway? I'm not hers, after all, she's got two of her own, even if one of them is a bit non-functioning. She's got no call to welcome me, and I don't trust it. If there is one thing I can't stand, it's falseness. Ann said once, "Your father misses you. I'm glad for *his* sake."

Well, I ask you? What can you make of that?

Last time I went to Crowbridge was a few weeks ago, to pick up some of my tapes that were still there. It's true, the kids always seem pleased enough to see me, they hug my legs; but then I reckon anybody coming to the house is a treat to them. Young Kate will always be the way she is now, she can't develop any more, there's some long medical explanation for that; Ann and my dad say it won't make any difference, she's one of the family whether she develops or not.

Easy to say that *now*; they may think differently in twenty years' time. The one it's rough on, in my view, is young Andy; he don't know what's ahead of him. Anyway—none of my business. But, for that reason, they don't have a lot of visitors coming to the house. People fight shy. You know.

Well, I went down to pick up my tapes. The way you get to Dad's place in Ferry Road, Crowbridge, there's a really crafty short cut. Gives me a terrific feeling every time I use it.

As you get to the town, the main road from Galhampton turns left at the bridge, and then you have to circle right round Crowbridge on the perimeter road, across a pair of roundabouts, and then back into Warden Street. It's all a one-way system.

Whereas, if you take the cut down Dead Man's Lane, you are there in a brace of shakes.

It was Ann who first showed me the short cut; she's lived in the town before, see, and knows all its crannies like the palm of her hand. As you come down the hill, Pelican Hill, it's called, named from the pub up at the top, you have to watch out very, very sharply, because it's a little, inconspicuous turn, looks more like somebody's private driveway than a public road. And in fact there are two private driveways before you come to it, so you have to watch for the third entry, which is Dead Man's Lane. Why it's called Dead Man's Lane I don't know, and Ann doesn't know either. Some dead man long, long ago. Whatever he did, or what happened to him, must have been pretty impressive, for the lane to be called after him. It's queer that nobody seems to remember. The lane isn't at all long, maybe a quarter of a mile, and halfway along there's an acute left-hand bend. Lord help you if you meet somebody coming the other way, for—would you believe it—they've never made Dead Man's Lane into a one-way road, I suppose because so very few people actually know and use it. At the bottom end it turns into Rope Walk, and *that* leads into Warden Street, where you only have to turn right and there you are in Ferry Road. Saves all that circuit round the town.

But the thing is, you have to be really nippy, coming down Pelican Hill, to judge your moment and slip across in front of the opposing traffic, into that tiny little deep-cut entrance. It always gives me a terrific zing when I do it on the bike—one minute you are chugging down the main road, among the heavy traffic, buses, trucks going to the harbour, hundreds of tourist cars, then—zwoosh!—you are out of it all, zipping down between those high narrow banks, with close-packed trees and bushes making a tunnel of it, thick and dark, arching over your head. Round the sharp left-hand bend, holding your breath in case there's something on the other side coming towards you—which, up to now, there never *has* been —and then, like coming out of a tube, you are back in bright daylight, rolling into Rope Walk, which has little red-brick Victorian cottages on one side, with box-sized front gardens. On the other side there's old timbered storehouses and a car park. The whole trip along Dead Man's Lane takes only a couple of minutes—less, maybe—but there's a kind of nippy thrill about it—like surfing, or swallowing an oyster, or the Big Wheel.

I lie awake at night, sometimes, thinking about it. Funny, though—it's not *possible* to lie awake thinking about it for more than a moment or two: it always puts you to sleep. Better than counting sheep! The one really sure-fire soporific; it works every, every time. I've sometimes thought it should be possible to patent it, to those guys who do operations without anaesthesia, by hypnotising their patients; you get an awkward one who won't respond to hypnosis, you just take him down Dead Man's Lane a couple of times and then get him to go into recall. Of course he'd have to be able to ride a bike, that's one problem.

Well, the last time I went to Dad's house was a bit of a frost. Why, I still am not quite sure. I got there, Dad wasn't in yet, he took some dreary job, teaching at the local Middle School. Had to get what he could, as they wanted to live in the town. And he was off organising a botanical excursion, wouldn't be in for a couple of hours, though it was a Saturday.

I'm never going to get married. I just don't see all this adapting your life-style and habits to suit another person, because they want to live in a place. I'm going to set myself up in one room with all my electronic equipment—as soon as I'm able—and that will be that. Then I'll do what I want.

Anyway, I walked into the house in Ferry Road and the twins each came and grabbed a leg; then, after a while, Kate crawled off, in her dopey way, but Andy followed me wherever I went. He can talk the hind leg off a mackerel, that one.

I was hunting for my tapes, and, of course, they'd all been *put away*. I had a hideous job finding them, had to shift half the furniture in the downstairs rooms to get at them in the cupboards where they had been stowed. There's a million cupboards in that house—I reckon that's why Ann likes it so, she's got what I'd call an obsessionally tidy nature, she can't stand to see things lying about in the open; when the kids have finished playing, every block has to go back into its box, trucks into their garage, crayons into the tin, paint water emptied, paper stacked together—it's enough to give the kids hang-ups that'll last into their nineties, if you ask *me*. Which nobody does. Of course maybe when you are in your nineties you prefer to have the ballpoints all sorted into their separate colours. I wouldn't know.

Anyway Andy helped me shift the big couch, and the chests and other things so as to get at my tapes—he loved that, he thought it was a great game to drag all the furniture into different places. And I made a heap of the tapes, for Dad had said he'd put the bike on the car roof-rack and drive me back that night.

Ann had gone off round the corner to the little GoodBuy Supermarket which is all they have there, she said it was a good chance for her to go out while I was there to babysit, and she'd get her hair done at the same time.

Luckily Kate had fallen into one of her endless naps, I'd really hate to have to be responsible for *her*. Andy's no problem, I'll say that for him. He just chats along.

When I'd got the tapes sorted out I was hungry—hadn't had any breakfast before I started out from Mum's—so I went and took a look in the fridge. Got out some pizzas and some chops and some other things that were there, and stuck them in the microwave. And ate the lot. Plus a big tub of buttercandy ice-cream, and a cake and some ginger buns that I found in the pantry. Moving all that furniture about had really hollowed me out. I asked Andy if he wanted any, but he said no, they'd only just had their lunch when I got there. At two o'clock! I ask you!

Then I remembered I wanted to make some shelves for my bedroom back at Mum's, so I went into Dad's workshop and found a couple of boards, and brought them into the kitchen, where it was warmer—I don't know how Dad can stand that cold workroom of his—and sawed them up. Andy loved watching that. He wanted to try sawing, but of course I wouldn't let him. But I let him play with the sawdust. He made it into patterns on the carpet.

While I worked, I was telling him about coming down Dead Man's Lane.

"*I* know Dead Man's Lane," says Andy, "we go that way when Mum takes us to the Bluebell Woods. Up Dead Man's Lane, up Pelican Hill. At my school they sing a song about Dead Man's Lane."

Andy goes to school though he's only five. Kate doesn't, of course, and never will. But I reckon Ann is glad to get one of them off her hands for a few hours.

"What's the song?" I say to Andy, thinking maybe it'll explain the name.

He sings:

"Dead Man, Dead Man, in Dead Man's Lane,
Tell me once, tell me again,
Tell me all I want to know,
I'll be your friend if you do so.

Three times, three times round
Drive three times round the town
Then down Dead Man's Lane you go
And he'll tell you all you want to know."

The tune, sung in Andy's droning little voice, was a bit like Baa Baa Black Sheep. I get him to sing it again, then I join in, and we have a real good time. Kate never wakes.

In the middle, Dad comes back. I suppose by now it's about half past five. He seems a bit annoyed—what about I can't make out—and then Ann comes back, and he lights into her because tea isn't ready. Ann's your silent sort, she never says anything, just puts on a kettle—it boils right away, and screams like a banshee because I'd had it on, just before, to make a big jug of coffee and choc mixed.

"I'll just go out for a few things," Ann tells Dad, looking rattled, and out she goes again. Dad stumps about—spreading sawdust everywhere—and says nothing either.

So I listen to a few of my tapes till Ann gets back, and then Dad says, "While she's making a meal, I'll take you back." That surprises me, as I thought I was to spend the evening there, but, OK, I collect my stuff and take it out to the Escort.

Kate's still asleep, but I say goodbye to Andy—Ann's in the kitchen frying chops, she gives me a kind of wave with her face turned away over the cooker—and then we slam off in Dad's car with my bike on the roof. And he gives me this long saga about working harder at school.

I don't listen to him much because I know perfectly well that I'm going to be all right. I'm absolutely sure of that. I do remember, though, to get the extra quarter's allowance out of him, though he's pretty glum and surly about it.

"What do you want it for?"

I owe a couple of the fellows, I tell him, and he's glum about that too.

"And when you do come down here—I wish you'd be more considerate to Ann—"

That really knocks me. "What did I do wrong, for Sam's sake?"

He just shrugs. And I begin to think the trip to Paris is off. But no, he still refers to it. Only if I pass the exams. And he wants me to come down to Crowbridge the week before. "That way," he says, "you can get some revision done in peace without all those friends of yours hanging around."

Well, OK; I don't argue. By then I'll have got the special pen—warranted to work, never fails—and some more of the stuff, the powder. Power powder, they call it. You sniff it—a little, but not too much, specially before a bike ride. Never too much.

So I say goodbye to Dad, and he drives off at top speed, as soon as I have my things out of the car, because he's always dead scared of running into Mum.

He seems a bit sad. I never know what he's thinking.

And that night, when I go to bed, I remember Andy's little rhyme: "Dead Man, Dead Man, in Dead Man's Lane . . ." and I say it over and I'm off to sleep as quick as blowing out a match.

So now it's the week before the exams, and I'm on my way back to Crowbridge. A dull, rainy afternoon. And, as I come to the top of Pelican Hill, I remember the rhyme again. "Three times, three times round, Drive three times round the town . . ."

Just for laughs, I think, I'll *do* that. Three times round the circuit of the perimeter road—it'll be a game to see how fast I can get around Crowbridge, I'll check the speed on my digital radio—up the hill again, round the roundabout at the top, then, zing! back down the hill, and into Dead Man's Lane.

So that's what I do.

First circuit takes four-and-a-half minutes; by the second I've cut it to four. Third in slightly under four, I'm really getting the feel of it now. Up the hill in a rainy streak, round by the old Pelican pub—then down again, with the air cutting away from me in bow-waves that you can almost *see.*

Across in front of the traffic—there's some braking and skidding, but not from *my* front wheel, which clips neatly in between the high entrance-banks of Dead Man's Lane—and now we're hurtling, we're zooming down the green tunnel, through the smell of wet green leaves and mud.

And now we come to the left-hand bend—and round beyond it I believe the Dead Man is waiting, waiting to tell me all I want to know . . .

The End of Silence

It was after Ma died that our father acquired the owl, and we started to hate him.

She was killed by a bomb. It happened at Frankfurt airport, when she was on her way back from a visit to Aunt Ginnie. "Goodbye, see you next Saturday, I've left enough cooked food in the freezer for a week, and I'll try to bring back some German rock records," she had said, when she left, six days earlier, and that was the last time we saw her. Death is extremely shattering when it comes baldly and unexpectedly like that; if somebody is ill, or in hospital, you have a little time to adjust, a little time for your mind to prepare. But in such a situation as ours, no way. I know this sounds obvious, but when you yourself are the victim, the truth of it really hits you.

We were all knocked out in different ways. My sister Helen went silent. I began addictively eating tortilla chips and reading murder mysteries. Bag after bag of chips, book after book, two or three a day. I got them from the local library or bought secondhand paperbacks from the Old Bus Station Wholesale Goods Mart. "You'll get horribly fat if you don't stop," Helen broke her silence to say. But I couldn't stop. Reading was a drug that numbed the pain.

Father came out worst. He went silent too, and lost a couple of stone in weight. Then he suddenly announced that he was sending us to boarding school.

His explanation *sounded* reasonable.

"I'm a writer, damn it! I've got to support us all and keep up the mortgage payments. My inventive faculty has to keep functioning, which is hard enough in present circumstances, Lord knows. How do you think I'd manage if I had to keep remembering about things like fetching you from school and stew for dinner?"

Ma would have managed somehow, if she'd been the one who was left, I thought but didn't say. Helen pressed her lips together and stared at her feet and then turned and walked away.

Apart from the shock of losing all our friends and familiar surroundings at one sweep, the boarding school wasn't too bad. People knew what had happened to us and were kind without making a fuss. Our connection with Father was a help, I suppose. He is fairly well known because, besides being a poet and an expert on Anglo-Saxon, he wrote that book about Alfred and the Danes, *The King's Jewel*, which they did on television and it was very successful.

Which was one reason why we took his excuses for packing us off to boarding school with more than a pinch of salt.

"He just wants to get rid of us," I said, "because we remind him of Ma."

"Well—he does have to look ahead," Helen argued. "One TV success won't last for ever. And it's four years since he wrote the *Jewel*. I'm sure he isn't doing any work. He just goes into the study and sits. I've seen him, through the window."

"That's why he doesn't want us at home. He's afraid we'll ask what he's working on."

When we went home for Christmas, there was the owl.

Aunt Joe had given it to Father. She's a vet, and someone had brought it into her surgery with a hurt wing, probably done by a car. "Your father needs something to look after," she told us. We would rather it had been us.

Walt Whitman was the name Aunt Joe had given the owl. It was a big bird, a pale barn owl, about a foot high, large as a cat, with a fawn-coloured back and skull feathers ending in a sort of Venus peak over its eyes. The rest of its feathers, front, face, and under-wings, were snowy white. The eyes were huge, black, and staring. I suppose it was a handsome beast, really, but we hated it. We felt it had supplanted us. There was something spooky and startling about its habits—you never knew where you would come across it suddenly, in the airing cupboard, or staring at you from the top of a bookshelf, or the handlebars of Helen's bike, or the kitchen dresser, or the oven. The oven and the medicine cupboard were two of its favourite spots.

"It's not hygienic!" Helen stormed at Father, but he said, "Rubbish. Owls are very clean creatures. And Whitman has completely cleared this house of mice. There isn't one in the place nowadays."

That was true. Mice had been a problem before. You do get them in old houses.

Whitman spent a lot of time in Father's study, perched on top of a bust of the poet Edgar Allan Poe. And because of this, Father insisted that we always knocked before going into the study—"So as not to startle Whitman."

"Really I bet it's to give Father time to look as if he's been working," Helen muttered.

But Father insisted that the owl *helped* him to work; its soundless presence in the room was an aid to concentration, he explained. I remembered that he used to say the same thing of Ma. "The only person in the world whose being in the room didn't prevent me from thinking," he had said about her, and sometimes he called her "My gracious Silence".

The owl affected our life in a good many ways. The landing window had to stay wide open at all times, rain or fine, hot or cold (and at Christmas it was *very* cold) for Whitman's comings and goings. The TV had to be turned off at ten sharp because, Father said, Whitman didn't care for the noise and vibration. Our friends with dogs were severely discouraged from coming to the house; in fact our friends were discouraged altogether; Whitman, said Father, didn't care for a lot of laughter and voices, or thumps and pop music, or smells of sausages and chips cooking. Whitman didn't like Helen practising the cello, according to Father, and he simply hated the sound of my trumpet.

"That bloody owl's just an excuse not to have us in the house at all!" Helen burst out one evening, close to furious tears because Father wouldn't let us give a party.

"Helen! I will not be spoken to like that! In any case I don't know how you can have the heart even to think of giving a party so soon after Marian—" His voice dried up and he sat staring at Helen with what seemed like hate.

"Don't you see, you silly man, it's because we want to take our minds *off*? How can we do that, when we have to tiptoe about all the time as if the place was an—an Intensive Care Unit?" And then Helen rushed out of the kitchen and up to her room, slamming doors all the way.

And Whitman, disturbed, left his perch on the plate rack and ghosted about the house on great pale wings, as if blown by an invisible gale.

Father simply stared at the calendar, obviously willing the last week of the holidays to go by at double-quick speed.

When we came home at Easter it was the same, only worse. Whitman was plainly fixed with us for life. Father had formed the habit of buying him little delicacies at a pet shop: foreign mice and lizards, things like that. The owl was more relaxed in our house; he made more noise than he had at Christmas, suddenly let out a weird shriek every now and then, which could startle you almost out of your wits. Or he would do a kind of loud snore, also very disconcerting, or suddenly snap his beak together with a loud click. He was not a restful house-mate. Despite this increase in vocal activity Father had, to our discomfort, begun to address the owl as Silence. Whitman, he said, was a silly name, not suitable, not dignified. Besides, Whitman was a silly poet. Silence was much more suitable.

All the old rules and regulations were in force, and some new ones too. Transistors were totally banned, so was playing table tennis. Father was afraid that Silence might get over-excited and swallow one of the balls, which could kill him.

"I wish it would," said Helen furiously. "If Father were to *marry* again, I suppose I'd hate it, but at least it would be possible to understand, and sympathise, because he's lonely and—and unfulfilled; at least that would be *natural.* But to be tyrannised over by a beastly *owl*—that's just absolutely *un*natural and spooky—it's like something out of those Poe tales that Father used to read us."

In the old days, when Ma was alive, we all used to read aloud to each other quite a lot; now we never did any more. I daresay, if pressed, Father would have been able to come up with some reason why Whitman—Silence—wouldn't like it.

"Do you think we could kidnap Whitman?" I suggested. "Pick a time when Father's out of the house, put the beast in a basket, and take him off on our bikes to some distant spot, and leave him there?"

"We could try," said Helen.

So we tried. We rode twenty miles—to Cranfield Forest—and left Whitman on an oak stump.

He was home before we were. So that was no good.

"Owls are very place-oriented," Helen said. She had been

reading about them in the bird book. "They use the same nest year after year. Obviously Whitman looks on this house as his nest now . . ."

"Well then I think we have to murder him."

"*Murder* him!" Helen looked aghast; but then she looked thoughtful.

For days we went around without speaking; we were all of us obsessed by the owl, one way or another. The awful thing was that he did, in some way, remind me of Ma; there was something about his pale face and widow's-peak brown cap and great dark eyes that somehow called up her face, but in a teasing, horrible, unreal way. I suppose that may have been at the bottom of his fascination for Father.

I spent hours racking my brain to think of some foolproof way to get rid of the owl. It would have to be done without the least chance of arousing Father's suspicion, or the results would be dreadful: he'd probably kick us back to school and forbid our coming home at all, send us to labour camps in the holidays and never speak to us again. But really, for his welfare as much as ours, I thought the deed must be done, only how? Poison, for instance, was out of the question; anything of that kind would point to us.

One night, after thrashing about wide awake for hours, I got up long before dawn. I sat hunched on my wide window-sill, gazing out. Our house lay on the edge of the town and beyond our garden hedge was a big hundred-acre field of young winter wheat, beginning to grow thick and green; beyond that lay a little wood. The sun, on the right, came up into a dim red cloudy sky like a thin melon-slice of blazing gold; into this theatrical light came a buoyant flitting shape which I soon recognised as Whitman, methodically quartering the wheat-field for breakfast. He flew quite silently, coasting with very little effort; then, sometimes, suddenly dropped with a wild flapping of wings. I've read that a barn owl can bring back a mouse to the nest every fifteen minutes. I don't think Whitman caught as many as that; but then he had no chicks to feed. The situation was unnatural for him too. Seen flying, his body looked wedge-shaped, and the wide pale wings looked almost translucent with the marmalade-coloured sunlight coming through them. And then, Mother's face looking out between them, when he turned his big black eyes in my direction . . . He has *got* to go, I thought, though at that moment I felt quite sad about it; he was so handsome, coasting to and fro in the early light that, just then, I felt a kind of sympathy with Father. All the same, he has to go, or we shall end up stark crazy.

It was at that moment I had the idea how to do it.

Father was due to go up to Edinburgh that day, to receive an honorary degree from the university. No cash in it, just bags of honour, he said rather drily. Still, it would be beneficial for him to get away, the first time he had done so since Ma's death, and he would stay a night in Edinburgh and return the following day.

He gave us endless instructions.

"Don't forget to lock up, last thing. And make sure all the lights are out. And mind you leave the landing window open, so that Silence can fly in and out."

At least we didn't have to worry about feeding Silence; he was a pet who provided his own diet, to do him justice. Though I didn't doubt Father would bring him back some fancy tit bit from Scotland, Celtic mice or Caledonian lizards. Whitman's presents at Christmas had far outnumbered ours, which consisted of an obviously last-minute chemistry set and paintbox.

Father left only just in time because road-works were in progress along our stretch of lane: a new water main was being laid, there were men with drills and a great excavator and a stretch of muddy trench on one side of the road, and a long lumpy ridge where the completed ditch had been filled in. The sound of the digger and the pneumatic drills had been steadily coming closer for the past three days; Whitman hated it, and so did Father; he was really delighted to get away to Edinburgh, and particularly today, when the work would be right outside our house. In fact if he had delayed his departure by another ten minutes the men would have dug their trench right across our garage entrance and he would have had to make his journey by bus and train.

We never kissed each other for greetings or farewells any more. "Behave yourselves," Father called, flapping his hand out of the car window, and then he drove away quickly, under the snout of the digger, which was just getting itself into position.

"Where's Whitman?" I said to Helen, as we put away the breakfast dishes.

"In the pantry. Why?"

"I've had the perfect idea. Come on: we'll do it now, and then we'll go out for the day. Take a picnic to Bardley Down. The house is going to be unbearable all day, anyway, with that row outside."

We found Whitman dozing on the pantry top shelf. He did that most of the day, sometimes snoring, as I have said.

By now he was quite used to us, and only snarled and grunted a bit as I picked him up and sat him in the gas oven, on the lowest rack, having taken out the others. Then I shut the door and turned on the gas.

After that, feeling like murderers—as we were—we grabbed some cheese and apples, locked front and back doors, and fled from the place.

"There won't be any sign of how he died," I said. "Father

can't possibly guess. He'll probably think Whitman died of old age. After all, we have no idea how old he is."

"Father will be horribly upset," Helen said wretchedly.

"Maybe that will be good for him."

"Just so long as he doesn't go and get another owl . . ."

We had a ghastly day. It was cold and cloudy, not quite raining, but raw; we had brought along books in our packs, but it was too cold to stop and read them, so we walked and walked, in a huge circle, and ate our lunch standing, in a big yew forest where the trees gave us a bit of shelter, leaning against one of the big reddish trunks. At one point we heard the unmistakable screech of an owl—"Yik, yik!" in the gloom.

"Whitman would have liked it here," Helen said sadly.

"It's no use, Nell. You know he'd only have come boomeranging back. We did try . . ."

At last, more dead than alive, we limped home ourselves, just as dusk was beginning to fall.

We had planned what to do: open doors and windows to let the gas escape, then retreat to the greenhouse for twenty minutes. The greenhouse was kept at an even temperature by an oil heater; it was the first time we had been warm all day.

"The gas ought to have dispersed by now," I said finally.

So we went cautiously indoors and flung open lots more windows. I turned off the gas and opened the oven door just a crack. I didn't look inside the oven. Hadn't the heart. Thought I'd wait till morning.

"I'm going up to bed," I said. "Don't feel like supper."

"Me too. Is it safe to go to sleep, though?"

"Open your bedroom window wide. And don't go striking any matches."

We crept to bed. I had expected to lie awake, racked by guilt and horror at the deed we had done. But I didn't; I slept as if I had been karate-chopped.

It was Helen who lay awake. When she came down in the morning I was alarmed: she was whiter than Whitman's shirt-front.

"Ned! *Whitman has been haunting me all night!*" she croaked. "He's been perched on my bed-rail."

"Oh, come on!" I said. But I was pretty scared myself —not of ghosts; I thought Helen was having some kind of breakdown. She looked so white and wild and trembling that I wondered if I ought to call the doctor.

"He made me think of Mother!" Helen wept. "Oh, Ned —why in the world did we do it?"

Just then Whitman—or his ghost—came coasting into the room on silent wings.

"Keep him away—keep him off me!" Helen shrieked.

Whitman made for the oven—the door of which stood open. And that made me realise for the first time that there was *no corpse inside.*

"It's all right, you dope—he's *not dead.*"

At that moment there came a peal at the front door.

"Gas inspector," said the man who stood there. "I've come to reconnect you and check."

"Reconnect—?"

"Didn't you know? The excavator cut the gas main yesterday. All this row of houses were cut off. Hey, what the blooming—?"

He had suddenly come face to face with Whitman, sitting in the oven.

"Oh, that's our owl," I said, weak and idiotic with relief. "He, he likes sitting there."

"Pretty stupid, dangerous place to let him sit," said the gas man. "Unless you fancy roast owl."

And he went about his business of reconnecting and testing.

That day we stayed at home. Our spirit was broken. We endured the hideous row made by the excavator and the drills —a few yards farther along, now; we did our school holiday work and washed some clothes; I mowed the lawn, Helen made a shepherd's pie against Father's return. That meant turning Whitman out of the oven. Restless and displeased, he found himself a new perch on the front hall coat-rack. I suppose being shut inside the oven had insulated him nicely, the day before, from the noise of the drills and the thuds of the digger.

"I hope they don't cut the gas main again," said Helen. "I'm dying for a bath."

At tea time, Father came home. Cross and tired, he flung open the front door—and Whitman flew out, straight into the jaws of the excavator. One crunch, and he was done for . . .

Father and Helen wept in one another's arms.

"He was so like Mother," she sobbed. "He had just her way of looking at you and not saying anything—"

"Yes, yes, I know, I know—"

Father didn't blame us. How could he? The death of Silence was nobody's fault.

But of course we feel just as guilty as if we had really murdered him. After all, we meant to; it was pure chance that our intentions came to nothing. We really are murderers.

Helen seems to have washed away her guilt in tears, and in looking after Father. But I haven't: I suppose because the gas oven was my idea. And I suppose it is because of that guilt that Whitman haunts me and not Helen.

Night after night, there he is, perched on my bed-rail, silent, motionless, staring at me with Mother's eyes. Whether I'm at school or at home, it makes no difference. Nobody else sees him.

Strangely enough, I'm starting to grow rather fond of him.

My Disability

Well, my dear, at first we couldn't even get *on* to the boat, because those fools of organisers hadn't seen fit to check on the one-way streets in Stjøck, or whatever the name of the god-forsaken port is—Stjøck was the word, I can tell you, there we sat, in our coaches, at ten in the evening, for three-quarters of an hour, if you'll believe me, while they went to request permission from the harbour master to take us down a hundred yards to the dock-side. Permission refused. I was obliged to give Herbert a piece of my mind, as I had packed some biscuits and a flask of tea in my on-plane bag, but dear Herbert, just like him, had put that bag with the other things in the coach luggage-hold, and of course we were not allowed to get out. Too much traffic in the street. And then, my dear, the coaches had to back up the hill and go a long way round, and we had to *walk*, half a mile at least, in the snow, for it was snowing, along the dock-side, climbing over and around every kind of rope and barrel and crate and capstan, or what-ever name they give those things. Imagine! And me with my disability, you can figure for yourself how I felt.

So then, at long last, we came to our ship, the *Queen of the Fjord*, ha ha, and I can tell you she didn't look much in the dark.

There were a couple of girls, they can't have been more than eighteen, welcoming us on board. Herbert gave them the glad eye, naturally.

"The wine will soon be open," they kept saying. "Join us

in the bar. We are just getting the wine off the ice now."

"It would be more to the point," I told Herbert, "if they put a kettle on the gas for a nice cup of tea or coffee."

"Well, you've got that flask you kept asking for on the bus," he said—most unreasonably.

"My dear Herbert," I said, "you can't expect me to drink that *now*; it will be cold by this time." Which it was.

First of all we went to find our cabin. My dear, it was no bigger than a dog-kennel. Not a single hook to hang our coats on. Only two coat-hangers in a wardrobe the size of a golf bag. One forty-watt bulb in the middle of the ceiling and, of course, the bedside lights did not work. No drawers; nowhere to keep my tatting and sewing kit—let alone underwear and Herbert's socks. "You'll have to get the cabin steward to bring us some more hangers and see to those lights," I told Herbert.

"Let's go up to the bar first," he said—like a man; so, naturally, I said no more.

Up we went, and, though they had a few bottles and were opening them, need you ask, my dear, it was only *red* wine. Poison to me, as you know. "You'll have to make them get some white," I told Herbert. But he only said, "All in good time. Have mineral water for now." He was busy chatting up the bar steward and the two hostesses, both blondes, who were passing round sandwiches. Not proper sandwiches, needless to say—they were that open-topped kind the Scandinavians go in for, with olives and prawns and bits of fruit rolling off the ham and cheese in every direction; a thoroughly messy way of eating, I call it. Specially standing up. Smorgasbord? More like *over*board. Bits were being squashed underfoot wherever you looked. We went off to bed very soon.

Breakfast was continental and did *not* impress us. I'd had

a bad night. I hate duvets: either you are too hot and suffocate, or the thing falls off and you freeze to death.

Plainly they were not used to people asking for tea, though they did produce it in the end, with an ill grace. (And—after a day or two, mark you—they found a box of cornflakes for Herbert.)

We had set sail overnight—another black mark for the management, since we never did manage to get a look at the town where we embarked—and were already steaming up this fjord, Skripsøfjord, or something. I must say, my dear, that fjords leave me cold, absolutely cold. See one, you've seen them all. Steep, bleak sides, sweeping down into the black water at an angle that gives you toothache, mountain peaks so high above that you get a stiff neck craning up to look at them. Trees, what there are, nothing but evergreens and those scrubby little larches; every now and then some great bird goes flapping overhead or suddenly smacks down into the water after a fish.

Fish! Don't speak to me of fish. We had it at every meal —smoked fish, pickled fish, dried fish, baked fish, fried fish. *Eel.* Have you ever eaten eel, my dear? *Don't start.*

On the first day we met our three guides, who would be looking after us on boat excursions, or coach trips ashore (in the parts where there were *roads*, that is).

My dear, two of the guides were *girls*, called Anni and Christa, both blondes. "We'd better pick the man," I told Herbert. "A man would be more use if anything went wrong." So we picked Jürgen—or Yurg, as everybody called him. He was a big, hefty, red-faced fellow, with a pale-yellow thatch of hair. Almost white it was really, looked odd above his red shiny face. But he was full of jokes, always a laugh, always chatting up the lady passengers—widows, mostly, there were more women than men. But Yurg had his jokes with the men, too—mostly over an aquavit in the bar.

"So: we go to look for the lost island," he told Herbert one day. "That will be our goal on this trip."

"Lost island, what lost island?" said Herbert. "No one told *me* about any lost island. I thought it was all ornithology and archaeology."

"Ach, only my joke. It is a folk tale, a legend. Up at the head of Skripsøfjord, seventy miles from the sea, is an island where trolls inhabit."

"Trolls?"

"They fly through the air, so goes the legend, carrying bundles of logs," said Yurg. "And they have power to change their shape. But mostly their shape is to have three heads, and blue scales, and to give off cold, as a furnace gives off heat. And they hate all noise, that is the only thing that annoys them."

There was a little boy, Ollie, on board, who happened to be in the bar just then, sitting with his parents, Professor and Mrs Kendrick, drinking orange squash and listening to this conversation. A nasty spoiled little wretch he was, my dear, the only child on the ship, indulged in every way, and always butting into other people's affairs.

"They eat humans, Trolls do!" he squeaked out. "Suck them dry, like oranges!"

"That is so," agreed Yurg, giving little Ollie an ironic nod.

"But what about the lost island?" Herbert persisted.

"Ach, well, mostly it is not to be seen. Only when the Trolls choose. Only one group in sixty or seventy will come across it."

"Because of fog, most likely," said Herbert. "There's always some rational explanation for these folk tales. Can one land on the island? It must be a great bird sanctuary."

"One can land when it is there, certainly," bowed Yurg. "Otherwise, instead, we visit a famous cave with bats, where you can go in the boat."

"Bats? Thank you *very* much," I said. "I'll sit that one out."

If there is one thing I cannot abide, it is bats.

The first twenty-four hours, we never disembarked at all; just went on chugging, on and on, endlessly up the fjord. Didn't see much other water traffic. Very occasionally there'd be a fellow fishing; or a ferry, with a few people in it, crossing from side to side, from one dismal little settlement of wooden houses to another on the opposite shore.

"How people can live here!" I said to Herbert. "And why bother to cross? It's the same on both banks."

"I suppose people were born here," he said. "And are used to it. Must be pretty quiet in the winter."

"Winter?" I said. "It's winter now!"

"Nonsense, my dear. Only October."

It certainly was quiet. As if everything were settling down for its winter sleep. Just sometimes the crawk of a bird. Herbert, of course, was wild about *them*. Anything with wings he saw, out would come the field-glasses.

He got very riled with little Ollie.

"Mr Wilcox, Mr Wilcox!" the boy kept screeching. "Look this way, *quick*! A huge bird with a red breast!"

And, of course, every single time Herbert got there, no bird to be seen.

"It had a red breast and a white tuft on its head," Ollie would tell Herbert. "And it was as big as a chicken—bigger!"

"The sort of bird best eaten with a pinch of salt," *I* said.

For little Ollie, as well as being truly obnoxious, was a born liar. The tales he told of life in Shrewsbury! To hear him, you'd think his parents were like royalty in the town. The only true bit appeared to be that he was a chorister in the Abbey choir. His mother did confirm that.

"He's got a lovely voice," she said, rather sadly. "The pity of it is, he's under strict orders from his choirmaster not to sing *at all*, outside of services and choir practices."

So we had to take little Ollie's voice on trust. And were happy to do so.

On account of my disability, I didn't want to move around the ship much. Mostly after breakfast I'd establish myself in the lounge bar, which had comfortable banquettes—I'll say that for the *Queen of the Fjord*—I'd fix myself up snugly with my tatting, and stay put there till lunch, while Herbert took pictures of the birds. After a bit, people got not to notice me much. I was part of the fittings. And, my dear! the gossip I picked up! That Yurg was having a fling with *both* the girls—Anni and Christa—that the captain was under notice, because he'd got drunk on the previous trip and lost the anchor; that the water supply was liable to run out soon and we'd have to spend a day at one of the fjord-side villages, refilling; that there was no radio-phone on board, the only way to get in touch with the cruise management, in emergency, would be to stop and phone from a call-box on shore.

"And there are such a *lot* of those!" I said sarcastically to Herbert, who shrugged. He was quite enjoying himself; in his way.

Meanwhile we chugged on *our* way. Every now and then we'd stop at some small, solitary anchorage, a pier built from huge chunks of granite, sticking out into the black, seemingly bottomless water. And there would be launches waiting, or a couple of coaches, ready to carry us inland, first up a hideous steep climb, zig-zagging across the mountainside, then over miles and miles of desolate country, to feast our eyes on something the cruise organisers considered a prime treat—

a tiny wooden church, whose main claim to fame was that it had been built four hundred years ago and nobody had bothered to add to it or pull it down; or a waterfall; or a seventh-century tomb; or a glacier.

"Glaciers are only frozen rivers," I said to Herbert. "Why—just tell me why—would anybody want to travel three hours in a coach to look at one?"

With my disability, sitting in a coach for as long as that is no joke, my dear, I can tell you. Though at least the coaches were well heated—more than one could say of the ship—and Yurg did turn out to be quite a good guide, full of tales and jokes and odd bits of information.

He always, on all these trips, wore a medallion on a leather string round his neck. The medallion was made of leather too.

"Was given me by my fiancée, Helga," he told me. "She is a glove maker in the big city. All the time she is making beautiful, beautiful expensive gloves for the fashion houses. Very well-paid work! This medal she makes me for luck, for safety, for insurance, since I must travel so much. She makes me a St Christopher medal out of bits left over from the gloves. She is a very loving girl, my fiancée."

Doesn't stop you from carrying on with Anni and Christa, I thought.

"Why should a leather medal bring you luck?" Herbert asked.

"Glove leather: it is thought to be very strong luck. Any piece left over from a glove—that is certain to bring good fortune. And protection."

"But why?" Herbert persisted.

Yurg did not know. "It is just so," he said vaguely.

Here another passenger spoke up: Miss O'Mara, a history teacher from Dublin. She was a little silent, weedy spinster lady, who had never said anything, up to now.

"A glove is a sign of good faith," she said, blushing. "It is a very ancient token."

And she went on to give us a bushel of unwanted information about glove marriages, glove money, and glove contracts.

I pointed out to Yurg—who was looking bored, though he was nodding politely—that the leather string which held his medal was coming unstitched. I offered to mend it for him, so he took it off and gave it to me. I put it by for later, as my sewing kit was down in the cabin.

Well, after lunch—yet more fish—we tied up at one of those forlorn anchorages. Two coaches were waiting to take those who chose on another scenic journey to see a ship's grave. A *ship's grave*, I ask you! And yet another waterfall. Anni and Christa were in charge of the coaches. Yurg was going to escort a boatload on a trip up the fjord to look at some ancient rock-carvings, runic inscriptions and a picture of the goddess Freyja blowing her horn.

To my surprise, Herbert said he didn't want to go on any of these outings. As a rule, he's quite keen on a boat trip. But it was because—he told me later—little Ollie and his parents had opted for the boat, and Herbert couldn't stand the prospect of being stuck at close quarters with little Ollie for several hours.

"I'll just stay on the bank and fish," he said.

Well, of course, put Herbert by a loch or a tarn with a rod in his hand, he'll be happy for days. So I said no more. Mind, *I* wasn't too wild, speaking personally, about looking at runes and the goddess Freyja, but the boat trip, I thought, would make a change.

Off we went, leaving Herbert, quite contented, on the jetty. When he's fishing, he smokes his pipe. Other times I won't allow it, certainly never indoors. Well, dear, it's a disgusting habit, isn't it.

Turned out there weren't many candidates for the boat. Perhaps little Ollie had put others off as well as Herbert. But also there was a nasty, snuffly cold going the rounds of the ship; quite a few of our group chose to stay on board.

"All the more room in the boat!" says Yurg cheerfully, helping me over the gunwale. With my disability, getting in and out of boats can be a problem; but I had my rubber-tipped stick. And Ollie's father, Professor Kendrick, turned out to be quite gallant, and was a big help too. Between them, he and Yurg guided me to a comfortable seat in the roofed-in section of the launch.

We waved goodbye to Herbert and chugged off up the fjord, under those beetling cliffs. Professor Kendrick was telling little Ollie about the Viking ships, with birds' or dragons' heads carved on their stem-posts, setting out from these shores to ravage the coasts of southern lands. Little Ollie looked bored.

"Not surprising, is it, really, that the Vikings should want to go off exploring to warmer parts," I said to Mrs Kendrick. "You can see they'd want to get away from their homeland. The mystery is why they ever came back."

It was foggy weather, cold and gloomy and quiet. Slop, slop, went the water against the cliffs, as the boat's wake fanned out behind us. The sun hardly ever shone here, except when it was due east, at sunrise. Why would anyone take the trouble to carve runic messages on these rocks? You'd think they'd find somewhere more cheerful.

Drifts of fog shifted about. Far up above us a few gulls wheeled, at the top of the cliffs. Here, the rock rose up on either side, steep as a wall. But after a while we rounded a bend of the fjord and saw that it widened out quite a lot;

there were rocky islets scattered over a kind of inland sea, which was surrounded by snowy mountains. Nobody —not a single boat—within sight. I shivered, and was glad I'd thought to bring my second-best fur, the one with the thermal lining. On the boat, though, the engine kept us warm.

Ollie said to me impudently, "At least *one* of your legs won't feel the cold."

I gave him such a look!

"Hold your tongue, Ollie," said his mother, but without any real grit in her tone.

She was shivering too.

Now we came to one of the little islands which had a cliff dropping sheer to the black water; Yurg sidled the boat up alongside and we saw the carving of the goddess Freyja riding side-saddle on her brindled cat and blowing her horn; she was waving her hand, looked quite jolly and carefree. Below her was carved a kind of triple leaf, intertwined.

Yurg made some male chauvinist joke about her.

"You had better not have said that," remarked Professor Kendrick, studying the inscription alongside, the runic writing, which to me looked like a lot of triple Es, and some Rs and Ks made with three strokes.

"Oh, and why not?" says Yurg laughing.

"Freyja does not tolerate impertinence," says Kendrick. "She was a touchy goddess. When a giant was after her, he'd stolen Thor's hammer, and he offered to give it back in exchange for Freyja; the gods had a serious discussion about handing her over to this giant; Thrym, his name was; and Freyja became so furious that her neck swelled up and scattered her gold necklace all over the ground. The inscription here says:

Cattle die, all beasts with cloven hoofs
And beasts with pads,
All must die in the end,
But the death of a man
Who has insulted Freyja
Is terrible beyond belief.

"Hey, Yurg, doesn't that scare you?" squeaks little Ollie.

But Mrs Kendrick told him to shut up.

Then we went on to another island, where there was a carving of the god Thor fishing from a canoe for a serpent. At least that's what Professor Kendrick said it was. You had to take Thor and the serpent on trust. The canoe was clear enough. I felt sorry that Herbert wasn't with us. He would have liked Thor's fishing rod.

Then, suddenly, Yurg let out a bellow.

"What's up, you run out of fuel?" says Kendrick nervously.

"No, no, but we are in luck, such luck! For there is the lost island, it is visible today! There it lies, straight ahead, now the fog has cleared."

Yurg's hand is shaking so much with excitement that you'd think it was the Taj Mahal or the Pillars of Hercules he was pointing at, instead of an ordinary, dingy little island. To me it looked exactly like all the rest, just a pile of rock, with a few spindly trees and some reedy grass growing near the shore.

"Can we land on it, can we?" clamours little Ollie.

"If you wish," says Yurg.

So he edges the boat up alongside a kind of rough rock platform and ties it to a metal ring-bolt that somebody has, at some time, hammered into the stone.

"There is a cave on the island," says Yurg. "With another inscription. We go see."

"Count me out," I say. "You know how I feel about caves.

I'll just stay here, nice and peaceful, and keep an eye on the boat."

Yurg looked a bit doubtful at that.

"Is best we all stay together," he said. But I was firm. You have to be, sometimes, with those people. They may mean well, but they get above themselves. I had no intention of being pinched, in the cave, by Yurg.

So they went ashore, Yurg, Miss O'Mara, and the Kendricks.

I stayed in the boat, perfectly comfortable, and I won't deny that I seized the chance of a little shut-eye. When they go ashore, other people always take an amazingly long time over what they are doing.

I was woken by a sound.

What kind of sound? Lots of people asked that, but, my dear, it's hard to say.

It was like no other sound I've ever heard. A kind of a *stunning* sound.

As if there had been an earthquake, perhaps. And, in fact, some boulders did come rattling and thundering down the rocky slopes of the island. One hit the boat and made it rock.

Now what have those fools been up to, I wondered.

At that moment I saw them come running: Miss O'Mara, and the Kendrick couple, and little Ollie.

White and horrified-looking.

They flung themselves into the boat, and Kendrick cast off. Then he started the engine.

"Hey! Wait a minute!" I pointed out. "Where's Yurg? What about *him*? You can't go off and leave Yurg behind."

"Oh, be quiet, woman," says Kendrick—quite rudely. "Yurg can't come. We have to go and get help."

And he heads away from the island at top speed. It looks

to me as if he's more concerned with getting away than with getting help.

"What happened?" I ask again.

Ollie was crying and shaking, his mother white as a ghost, while Miss O'Mara had hunched herself up and was rocking to and fro over her crossed arms as if she had the pain to end all pains.

"The cave fell in," snaps Kendrick flatly. "Fell in on Yurg."

"Cyril, you know that's not true, that's not what happened," wailed his wife.

"What did happen?" I said again.

Miss O'Mara sobbed out: "Yurg set fire to himself with the candle. Oh, it was horrible! And then the rock fell in—"

"With the candle? How could he possibly do that?"

Little Ollie leaned over the gunwale and vomited. His mother promptly did likewise.

"Watch that wretched child!" I snapped—I can tell you, my dear, I was becoming very fed up with them all, and their idiotic stories. And *all* we needed, at this moment, was to have young Ollie topple into the fjord and someone be obliged to go after him. It certainly would not be me. I grabbed him by the scruff, held on to him till he had finished throwing up, and then shook him, none too gently.

"Come on, now, let's have a straight story. What happened?"

Little Ollie looked me in the eye and said, gulping, "It was a Troll. It was covered in blue scales, it had three heads and six arms. Blue flame came out of its mouths. It picked up Yurg and pulled his head off. It was coming towards us, but—"

"But what? What happened?"

"I sang," said Ollie. "Trolls hate noise. I sang a *Gloria*

that we've been practising in the choir. And the Troll turned round and went back, far back into the cave where it had come from. And then the roof started to fall, so we ran out. The Troll took Yurg's head with it."

"That, of course, is total rubbish," said Professor Kendrick, who had a white ring all round his mouth. He gave a furious look at his son. "I'll speak to *you* back on the ship," he said.

"Oh, be quiet, Cyril," said his wife.

"I think I'm going to faint," said Miss O'Mara.

Luckily I remembered that I still had some instant coffee in my flask. There was just enough for a small drink all round. After that, nobody said anything at all until we got back to the ship. Kendrick went straight off to the captain's office. The others made for their cabins, and I looked for Herbert.

He, my dear, was as pleased as punch, because he had caught two sea-trout and arranged to have them served for our evening meal.

After twenty minutes Kendrick came out of the captain's office looking irate. The captain sent for Miss O'Mara. Then for Mrs Kendrick. Then for me.

"Can *you* give me any account of this business, Mrs Wilcox?" he asked me.

"Not having left the boat, I can't," I said. "Only what the others told me. All their stories disagreed. Professor Kendrick's is the most likely to be true. There certainly was a rock-fall. I heard a loud noise, and some boulders fell. Are you going to send a party to look for Yurg?"

"I can't, in the dark," he said.

Of course dark falls early in those parts. It was dusk by the time we got back to the ship.

"Besides, we'll need a professional rescue team with helicopters," said the captain. "I have to telephone for that."

He went ashore to do so, from a kind of coastguard post at the anchorage.

That night the atmosphere on the *Queen of the Fjord* was like a funeral barge. Anni and Christa were both in floods. *I* thought about Helga, the girl who had made Yurg his medallion.

Herbert, who had never much liked Yurg, was the only cheerful passenger, because of his two trout. Several times during supper I was obliged to speak to him sharply, and once I had to kick him on the ankle.

Next morning the captain went ashore to phone again, and came back looking pale and startled.

He told Herbert—who told me—that the body of Yurg had been picked up, *ten miles away*, inland. At a place called Skenlønd, or something like that. Yurg was dead. And—this is the part that even Herbert found hard to swallow—his body was completely hollow, empty, deflated, like an orange that has been very thoroughly sucked. The head was separate.

The *Queen of the Fjord* turned round and steamed back to the port where we had embarked. Nobody mentioned Yurg. I still had his medallion, of course. The best thing to do seemed to be to drop it over the side, so that is what I did.

Only one person alluded to the episode. And that was little Ollie. He said to me, as Herbert and Professor Kendrick were helping me up the steps on to the plane that would take us to England: "Anyway, the Troll wouldn't have wanted *you*. Trolls don't eat people with wooden legs."

Toomie

When you travel with a ghost, your problems can be really acute.

Julia and I had hoped, of course, to get off to France without Toomie. But our hope was not even founded upon sand; it was founded on thin air.

As soon as plans for the summer holidays at Ste Baume leaked out, the demands began.

"Can we bring Toomie with us? Please—oh *please*!"

"We *can't* leave poor Toomie back at home. All on his own! That would be wicked!"

"She'd be so lonely!"

For a long time, it had been thought that Toomie was a boy.

"He wears boys' clothes," said Marianne.

"But that's because it's safer. He's really a girl. He told me so *himself*," argued Tom, who was two years younger.

"Why was it safer?"

"Because—because—people might hurt him," said Marianne. "His father used to beat and bang him *dreadfully*."

"But his own father must have known whether Toomie was a boy or a girl?"

"It wasn't really his father—it was only his—his—step-father."

Large areas of Toomie's life remained pretty vague. Julia and I felt this was just as well, for it had plainly been a short and unhappy one. Nor were we able to discover precisely when he had lived.

Tom said: "He's still alive *now*."

"No, silly, that's only his ghost," said Marianne. She frowned in thought. "When Toomie was here it was a very long time ago. In the war."

She could not tell which war.

"When there wasn't much food."

That might have been any war.

"We've told her about France. We've told him how lovely it is at Ste Baume. He really, really wants to come."

"She's never been in any other country but England."

Privately, Julia and I hoped that, when it came to the point, Toomie would be unable to leave Camberwell. Surely ghosts don't usually go abroad? But the drive to the airport showed that, so far, the migration presented no problem.

"You can sit between us, Toomie. But you can sit up on top of Tom's pack, so you'll be able to see out. Look, look at all the buses."

And, at the end of the flight, the lady who had shared their three-seat row in the plane said to Julia nervously, "It's really wonderful what imagination children have nowadays, isn't it? I suppose they learn to play these games at school?" before making off hastily into the airport with her hand luggage.

At the Lyons airport our trouble started.

Toomie, it seemed, was fascinated by the luggage carousel. As is always the way, our five large duffel bags were the very last to be extracted from the plane's hold, and in the meantime we had spent half an hour watching other people's wooden boxes, rolled-up mattresses, easels, outsize pink teddy bears, infra-red grills, and plaster peacocks whirling round and round on the conveyor belt, unclaimed, and apparently unrequired by their owners. The things that people take with them on their travels! But few of them, I thought, as unwelcome or as inconvenient as Toomie, who, according to Tom and Marianne, now hopped on to the belt, between the pink nylon ted and the infra-red grill, and was borne off through the flapping rubber fringe.

"Oh, TOOMIE! Come back!"

"What's the matter, Marianne?"

"Toomie's gone off with the luggage!"

"Don't worry, he'll come back in the other way," said Tom robustly. "Yes, look, there he comes. Oh Dad—can *I* do that too? Can I get on the luggage belt?"

"No, you certainly may not."

"But Toomie did."

"Toomie's a ghost. We aren't responsible for what he does. But you'd better tell him to get off. Any minute now our luggage will come through, and then we're leaving. Yes, look, there is one of the bags."

By the time all our bags had turned up, Toomie, it seemed, had fortunately had enough of riding the carousel and was prepared to accompany us to the car rental counter, where a great many forms had to be filled in. The children grew restless and impatient.

"Toomie doesn't like it here."

"Well, he'll have to put up with it, like the rest of us," Julia said shortly. "Do you want to go to the loo? Down those stairs."

Toomie, it seemed, was immune to such needs. One advantage of being a ghost. But when the children came back, they fell into panic and anguish.

"Where's Toomie?"

"I don't know," said Julia crossly. "Isn't she here?"

"No."

"No!"

"Toomie! TOOMIE! *Where are you?*"

At this moment the rental formalities were completed.

"Come on," I said. "Our car is in the car park, at the very farthest end. As usual. Everybody please carry one piece of luggage."

"*We've got to wait for Toomie!*"

"We certainly have not. If that ghost chooses to wander off, that's entirely his own concern. We have a four-hour drive ahead of us, I'm not waiting any longer or we shan't get there before dark. Come on!"

With Tom in tears and Marianne biting her lip, we humped our bags and struggled across the car park. Even Julia seemed concerned.

"Look—" she said. "I know it's all just—But if we start the holiday in such—I mean, it's going to be hard to—Well, I don't know exactly how we—"

Luckily, as we were ramming the last of our enormous bags into the tiny luggage compartment of the hired car, the problem solved itself.

"Oh, TOOMIE!"

"Where *were* you all this time?"

"We thought we'd *lost* you!"

"Will you please tell that ghost not to wander off any more," I snapped, as Julia stuffed the children into the back with drinks, biscuits, comics, books, and listening apparatus.

"He thought he saw Chap," Tom explained, as we threaded our way out of the airport complex and took the road south. "He hasn't seen Chap since he died. Chap, I mean. He's always looking for Chap."

"And who, pray, is Chap?"

There was a moment's silence while explanations were imparted.

"Chap was Toomie's dog. But he was killed. It was very sad."

"Something perfectly dreadful happened to Chap."

"What kind of dog was he?" Julia hurriedly asked, hoping to bypass any account of Chap's dreadful end.

"One of those dogs with flat, squashed-up faces."

"A bulldog? A Boston terrier?"

These terms, apparently, meant nothing to Toomie.

"He was brown."

"And quite big."

"Anyway," said Julia, "if Toomie is a ghost, and Chap is a ghost too, why can't they—well—get together?"

A long silence followed this reasonable-sounding question. At last Marianne said, "Toomie says it's not as simple as that."

"Nothing is ever simple," I sighed. "Look, Julia, can you just tell me which way I go at this hideous junction that's coming up ahead?"

She studied the map.

"You want to take the road to Annonay."

"There isn't one."

"St Etienne, then. Get quickly into the outside lane."

"Oh."

Luckily, after an hour or so, the children, tired from our early start, fell asleep.

Whether Toomie slept or not, we could not tell. He/she never talked to us.

The hills grew steeper, the villages smaller and more scattered, the roads narrower.

At last, when we were within a mile of our destination, the children woke, yawning, stiff and thirsty.

"Are we nearly there? Oh, good!"

The last mile to Mas Honorat is all downhill. Down a

single-track, narrow, precipitous, zigzag track, a dirt road which in winter becomes more of a challenge than any bob-sleigh course. The view is spectacular, but passengers in cars are seldom looking at it; they are watching the distance from the wheels to the edge of the track, or praying, or keeping their eyes on their laps.

Not Toomie, though.

"Toomie says he's never, *ever*, seen anything like *this*!"

"Well, that's nice," I said, feeling for the first time a faint warmth towards Toomie. Poor little south London brat, these French mountains must indeed be a surprise for him. Perhaps he/she had never been to the cinema. Perhaps he/she had lived before moving pictures were invented? Or photographs?

"Toomie says, what a good thing we brought the skate-board."

"You did *what*?"

I had been aware, in a vague way, at home, that Tom, who is one of the chief skateboard stars in his playground, had said sometimes, "Toomie loves to ride with me. They didn't have skateboards when she was alive. She thinks skateboards are really plummy."

If we had a language expert with us, I thought, we might be able to date Toomie's life in London from the use of that word plummy.

"Listen," I said, "I didn't know you were planning to bring the skateboard, and if I had known, I would certainly have forbidden it. Mas Honorat is no place for skateboards."

"But why, Daddy?"

"Look at the gradient."

Some of the zigzags were so sharp that I had to back the car down the next leg, as there was not sufficient room to make a proper turn.

"This track was made for mules, not cars or skateboards.

If you went off at the corner, you'd end up at the bottom, in the fleuve, probably with a broken neck. No skateboarding."

In fact, one of the first things I did when we arrived at the Mas, was to remove the skateboard from among Tom's T-shirts and perch it high, out of reach, on a beam in the unfinished area which would one day be the extra guest room. Mas Honorat had been constructed from the ruins of two farmhouses on different levels of the steep hillside, and it was far from complete. Half of each holiday we spent there was devoted to construction work.

While I was carting beams and mixing mortar and rolling rocks, Julia attended to the garden, which consisted of rockeries and tiny terraces, where grew such hardy plants as could survive deep snow in winter, roasting sun in summer, and the attentions of wandering deer and wild boar. Twice a day we took the children swimming in the river—which meant a five-mile detour down the valley and back the other side, in order to reach a spot that was exactly below Mas Honorat, only a few hundred metres down the prickly mountainside, but, from our side, inaccessible until we could afford to quarry ourselves a track down.

Toomie, it seemed, did not swim. Could not swim. Had never entered water in his/her life (even to wash? we wondered) and had no intention of starting at this stage.

After each of our swimming excursions the children were always a bit subdued for a while; it seemed that Toomie went into a sulk at being excluded from a pleasure we were all sharing.

"Though it is his own fault," Marianne said fairly. "I'm sure she could learn. It's silly of her to get so grumpy."

Back at the Mas, the children and their companion occupied themselves quite peacefully for long spells of time, while Julia gardened and I carried on my building operations. On previous holidays Tom had helped, or hindered me, mixing cement and trundling wheelbarrow-loads to and fro, while Marianne played quite a useful part in Julia's garden activities. But this year they kept strictly to their own affairs.

"Well, I suppose it's quite healthy in a way," Julia said, one evening on the terrace, as we drank wine and rested our aching backs, while the children, already in their hammocks, sleepily conversed or listened to the local radio station.

"I wonder if Toomie is picking up any French?" I said. "And what exactly do you mean by *healthy*? Is it really healthy to play with a ghost? I do worry about what he may tell them."

"Well, we've always said it was a pity there aren't any local children for them to play with. So I suppose in a way it's as well they have Toomie."

Ste Baume could hardly be described as a village. It was a community of scattered farms dispersed over many miles of breakneck slopes. Our nearest neighbour, Madame Berthezène, was within a hunting horn's distance as sound carried or the raven flew, but we were not ravens, and it took half an hour to reach her by car. She was an elderly widow in her late eighties, whose children, and even grandchildren, had long since predeceased her.

"Let's go and call on Madame tomorrow," Julia said. "I've masses of pictures for her."

Madame collected pictures of the English royal family, and we spent our winters chopping them out of newspapers and magazines. The Queen Mother was her special favourite. "Ah, quel courage! Quelle bonté!"

When we said we were going to call on Madame, the children, who usually adored her company, were unexpectedly reluctant.

"You'll only talk boring grown-up talk and drink horrible aniseedy drinks for hours and hours. Can't we stay at home?"

"Well—all right; if you'll be sensible."

For several days past they had been absorbed in a slightly incomprehensible game involving the use of a number of sawn-off rounds of tree trunk, fuel for the stove, which they used as stools, or stepping-stones, or building material. "*Don't* move that, please, it's Toomie's palace wall!"

"Oh, sorry. Must he have his palace right in front of the kitchen door?"

"It's the only flat place."

Well, that was true. But, otherwise, it seemed a harmless occupation.

Only once had I been obliged to issue a veto, when they began rolling the rounds of wood down the mountainside.

"Please stop that, it's dangerous."

"Why?"

"Well, firstly there's a bit of cliff below the house, you can't see who might be down at the bottom. People come there to fish. And no one wants a ten-pound log falling on his head. And, secondly, it took a lot of trouble carting these logs here. We don't want them wasted."

Tom took this prohibition in good part.

"Actually," he said, "it was Toomie's idea."

Toomie, apparently, went into another of her sulks.

"Toomie and Tom like playing boys' games," Marianne later confided gloomily to Julia. "It's not much fun for me with them any more. I'd rather help you with the garden."

"Well, when we come back from Madame's, you and I can plant a row of lettuce seedlings. She says she's got some to give me."

"Can I come with you?" said Marianne unexpectedly. "To Madame? I'd like to see her."

"And leave Tom on his own? No, I don't think that would be such a good plan."

"He'd have Toomie."

"A ghost isn't really enough company," said Julia.

In the car, on the way to Madame's house, she said, "And I'm beginning to think that Toomie isn't a good influence. I'm a bit anxious about what she tells them."

"*I've* thought that all along."

"I wish we could think of some way of getting rid of him."

"Me too," I said with feeling.

"But I don't suppose there's any chance of its happening in France. Perhaps when we get back to Camberwell . . ."

Madame was desolated not to see les petites anges. "I have been baking some special cakes for them. Well, you must take them when you go. But please, please bring Tom and Marianne to visit me very soon. Onyx is sad not to see them, also."

Onyx was her immense, blunt-faced brown mountain dog, reputed to have rescued several snow-bound travellers in the course of his long life.

We spent a pleasant hour with Madame, who was a kindly, massive lady, exuding bounty. But then she grew unexpectedly fidgety.

"No, I don't like it too much that you leave those [illegible] on their own. It is better you should return to them."

In fact we had been feeling the same way, and left her terrace readily enough. Mas Honorat was not visible from her ridge of the mountain.

"As a matter of fact, Madame, they aren't entirely alone," Julia explained, to give the conversation a more cheerful turn, for Madame's brow was furrowed with worry. "They have their ghost friend with them."

"Hein? Un revenant?"

Explanations about Toomie took quite a little while, during

which I was dying to get away. To my surprise, Madame received Julia's account with total seriousness.

"For myself, I have a complete belief in phantoms," she said. "I am a sensitive, you see, un médium, how do you say it in English?"

"A medium. Same word."

"After people die, sometimes it happens that the spirit lingers for a while, confused, lonely, uncomprehending. Then it longs for company. So that is why, doubtless, this sad little ghost has attached itself to your pair. But it is not a desirable relationship."

"No, *that* it isn't," I agreed. "But why do you think so, Madame?"

"Because it will be most natural that this ghostly *copain* may wish that one of the children, or both, should also become a spirit. So as to ensure permanent companionship. Whereas, of course, this Toomie should be working to free himself from all the ties that still attach him to this world and his former life. And travelling on to greater freedom."

"Yes, I see. And I quite agree."

"I wish you will go home *now*, at once," said Madame forcefully.

I drove as fast as I could; but you really cannot hurry on those tracks.

At the top of the drive down to Mas Honorat we met Marianne, looking tearful and distressed. She hurled herself into the car.

"I was coming to get you! Toomie has talked Tom into getting down the skateboard."

"But how could he possibly? How could they reach it?"

The ladder, I had taken care, hung high enough so that Tom, on his own, could not get it down.

"Oh, they are piling up those bits of log to make a staircase.

And then they are going to ride down The Slope. *Please* hurry, Daddy."

She was on Julia's lap, and I was feather-stitching my way down the zigzag with infinite, frantic, desperate care.

The Slope was what we called the forty-five degree angle of mountainside that connected all the zigs and zags of the track. A long, lethal slant of it lay above and on the far side of the house. I did not dare look in that direction, as I guided the car down on to its usual stopping place, but Julia suddenly said, "I can see them," in a voice so dry and faint that it sounded as if her throat were full of sand.

I leapt out of the car and shouted, "*Tom!* Stop that!"

"*Tom!*" screamed Marianne. "Toomie wants to *hurt* you!"

Julia had raced into the house. I could not think what for, until I saw her reappear, dragging the enormous beanbag which served us as a sofa on wet days.

"You brilliant woman!" I croaked, in a voice as dry as hers, and helped her shove and haul it up the dusty slope, and place it in the track of the oncoming Tom.

"*Wheeee!*" he was shouting. "Isn't this *plummy*! Hey, Toomie! We must be going a hundred miles an hour!"

The beanbag stopped them. Stopped Tom, and the skateboard, at all events.

Tom was considerably cut and grazed. But what really shook him was our passion, and our rage against Toomie.

"He didn't mean any harm. *Honestly*, Daddy. It was just a game."

"You are not to play with Toomie *any* more. At all. *Ever.* And I am going to chop up the skateboard and burn it."

Tom went weeping off to his hammock.

The atmosphere at Mas Honorat was dreadful.

"Toomie's terribly upset," Marianne told us. "And angry, too. He doesn't understand at all why you are so cross. And, actually, I don't see how you *can* stop Tom playing with her."

Nor did we.

"I'm going to go and see Madame," said Julia.

While she was gone, I carried out my threat, chopping the skateboard into firewood, removing its wheels, and stuffing it into the stove. While I performed these actions I felt surrounded by cold, malignant silence. It took no effort at all to imagine Toomie at my elbow, watching, speechless, furious, waiting his chance to do me a bad turn.

When Julia returned, Madame followed behind in her own car.

"In our hurry we forgot Madame's delicious cakes," Julia said, and took them into the children's room. A silence lingered behind her as she emerged; I hoped very much that it came from contented nibbling.

Madame sat upright in our wooden armchair. Onyx, who had accompanied her, placed himself with gravity, equally upright, beside her.

"Tell me again what happened," said Madame, and listened, nodding, to our account.

"It may well be, as Tom says, that the little revenant meant no *harm*, in our sense of the word, to Tom," she then pronounced. "After all, to him, death is no different from life . . . Eh, mon Dieu! Regardez Onyx!"

The monumental and dignified Onyx was lying on his back, waving paws in the air, an expression of idiotic bliss on his face.

"Toomie is rubbing his stomach," explained Marianne, who had come quietly from the children's room. And she added, in a low voice, "I believe Toomie thinks that Onyx is Chap."

"And who was Chap?" inquired Madame.

"Chap was Toomie's dog."

Madame nodded. "Who knows, maybe it was so? Who knows if dogs have souls too, and can come back? Maybe those two arranged, long ago, to meet here?"

She addressed the air.

"Toomie? Ecoute, mon enfant! You are now coming home to live with me, and Onyx. Comprends-tu?"

"Can you *see* Toomie, Madame?" whispered Marianne, awestruck.

"Almost," said Madame Berthezène, with her severe smile.

I knew what she meant. I myself had *almost* seen Toomie sitting on Tom's shoulders, atop of the skateboard.

Madame got up and left, Onyx following. We heard the sound of her car start and drive off.

Marianne went into the children's room and said, "Tom: Toomie has gone to live with Madame and Onyx."

A very long silence followed. Then Tom muttered, in a choked, tearful voice, "Well, perhaps it's a good thing. Madame always said she was sorry not to have children in her house. And we can always go and see Toomie when we come for the holidays."

I suppose that is true, I thought, with little enthusiasm.

But a cold, early autumn set in that year, after we had left Ste Baume at the end of August, and a ferocious, freezing winter. Blizzards and avalanches were frequent. One of the avalanches swept down the mountainside and removed Madame's house, with her inside it, Onyx, her furniture, and all her pictures of the British royal family.

"Perhaps she and Toomie and Onyx are all keeping each other company somewhere," Tom said sadly, when we received this news.

But I hoped that Madame, and Toomie also, had travelled on to a greater freedom. As she herself would have put it.

The King of Nowhere

The alarm clock whirred through the dark and Mado, still tired after a noisy and disturbed night, stretched out a hasty hand to silence it. With eyes still shut, she rolled out of bed, stood up, shuffled her feet into slippers (they all slept in trousers and sweater, those days) and moved off like a robot to the kitchen. It was freezing cold and tidy. They had a rule among them, firmly kept, that, because of probable night disturbances, the kitchen must be left orderly as a ship's bridge by whichever one of them was at home during the evening. The blackout blind was still pulled down, so Mado was able to switch on the light. Plus one, she thought to herself. She had a game of pluses and minuses for beginning the day. If the mail arrived before she left for work, if Matt came home, if she saw a cat on the way to the office . . .

A kettle stood ready filled; she lit the gas (another plus) walked along to the bathroom, washed and brushed her teeth (water in the taps; yet another plus) then returned to the kitchen, made tea, and let it draw while she took cups, milk, sugar, from the cupboard; then she carried the tray, yawning, into the living room where her younger brother slept on a divan.

The blackout was still in place here, too. She switched on the table lamp, lit the gas fire, and turned on the radio, which sighed out a sad little nasal minor-key tune, *Lazybones*, theme song of a morning music programme.

"La—azybones—sleepin' in the sun—How you spec' to get your day's work done—?"

Tom rolled over in bed, cocooning himself, resolutely turning his back on morning or tea or his sister.

"Come on, wake up!" she said. "You know you've got to. Anyway, it's Friday. Weekend tomorrow—"

"*And when you—go fishin'—I bet you—keep wishin', The fish wouldn't grab at your line—*"

Tom gradually turned over, uneasily, hostile, still subhuman, but reached out a skinny arm, took his cup of tea, and began drinking it. Mado sprawled, relaxed in her armchair, the fire puttered and purred gently, and presently an announcer gave them the war news.

After it was over, Mado cautiously undid the curtains, letting in a dim, frosty morning light.

"Come on now, get up, dormouse boy," she said. "I'm going to start breakfast. Dried-egg fritters on fried bread. I expect Matt will be home quite soon."

Her expectations of this were not so high as her voice suggested but, in fact, while she was mixing the dried egg powder to a thin paste with milk and flour, Matt, their elder brother, came in from night shift and sat on the kitchen table while she supplied him with tea and toast.

"No trouble here?" he said. "We spent half the night in Fleet Street putting out incendiaries."

"None very close." Mado sat down and bit into a piece of toast. "One fairly big one a few blocks north—in Marchmont Street, perhaps."

Tom came in wearing pyjamas and sweater, face red from scrubbing, hair up in damp spikes.

"'Llo, Matt. Where's mine? Isn't it dark? Hellish cold, too. We don't seem to get daylight any more. I'll be late tonight—sixth-form debating society."

"You're supposed to be *dressed* for breakfast." His sister handed him a plate of fritters.

"I *am* dressed." His tone was injured. He bolted the greasy food, washing it down with copious draughts of tea. "Is there another cup? Any marmalade left?"

"You finished it yourself."

"When does the new period start?"

"Monday."

"Oh, heck!" Morosely, he scraped a little brown sugar over his toast.

"And go easy with the marge."

"All right, all right!" Dumping his plate in the sink, he stomped out.

"Betty rang up," said Mado to Matt. "Asked how much longer you'd be on the night shift. I said you'd ring her back."

"She wants me to take her to a film."

"What's wrong with that?" asked Mado, surprised at his tone. "I thought you liked her?"

"Oh . . . too tired in the evenings. Rather come back here and listen to records. How's Andy? He OK?"

"Seems quite serene."

"Bombs begun to worry him?"

"No; I don't suppose they will. Why should they?"

"*I* dunno. Any more tea? Thanks. I'm off to bed. I'm going out at five; lecture on gas, effects of. But I'll be back by eight."

"Good. So will I. That means I needn't wash the dishes this morning. Tell Tom to hurry as you go past—he'll be late for school."

Mado dressed herself in office clothes and scanned the groceries cupboard. Then, as Matt had come out of the bathroom, she did her hair in front of its mirror and put on make-up.

Tom had clattered down the stairs already, swinging his school bag, shouting goodbye over his shoulder. Mado left

Matt slumping down on to the divan, and, bracing herself, went out into the winter day which was windless but raw, icebound, and misty. Although her office was only ten minutes' walk from the flat she had twice to make detours to avoid bomb damage. Wooden barricades were placed across streets, men were digging with picks and pneumatic drills; the air resounded with the clink of iron on stone. The building in which she worked had windows broken, and trees in the square outside it were shattered and splintered. As usual, Mado spent the first half hour of the working day sweeping grit and broken glass from the grey and battered parquet floor.

As she walked home in the dusk across Bloomsbury Square carrying a bundle of reports to read at home (nobody tried to work much after four, the office lights were too dim and flickering) Mado encountered her sister Joyce—tall, beautifully dressed, high heels, with a poodle on a long lead. Joyce must know someone who's just come from Cairo or New York, Mado reflected without malice, observing her sister's silk stockings.

"Hullo, Joyce. Doesn't he feel the cold, trimmed as short as that?"

"Mado. How extraordinary to run into you."

Joyce glanced distastefully at Mado's string bag, containing celery, a lump of butcher's offal wrapped in bloody newspaper, candles, bread, a bag of washing soda, and a tin of dried milk.

"Of course he doesn't feel the cold," she said impatiently. "He's used to it. How are the boys?"

"OK. Tom passed his middle-grade piano. Matt's on night shift."

"Tom ought to be in the country. Walter says—"

"I know, I know. Safe from bombs and in the nice fresh air. But you couldn't get him away from Lenkovic."

"Piano lessons! Someone could teach him in the country."

"It wouldn't be Lenkovic, though, would it?"

"It's unhealthy, you living in that dark flat with the boys. Walter says—"

"No darker than anywhere else. It's dark nearly all the time anyway."

"It's time you were married. Here you are, almost thirty—"

"Twenty-six," said Mado under her breath.

"And Matt twenty-eight—"

"He's got his dud lung to worry about."

"Walter says—"

"Let Walter worry about the destabilisation of the currency rather than our trifling concerns. Who is there to marry, anyway?"

"It must be lonely for you in the evenings," asserted Joyce, reining in the poodle, who wanted to investigate under a bush.

"One or two of us are mostly in. And there is always Andy."

"Who's Andy?" asked Joyce sharply.

"The lodger."

"*Lodger*, where do you put a *lodger*?"

"He sleeps during the day . . . in the living room."

"Drawing room," said Joyce automatically. An air-raid siren began to sound—a long, lugubrious, rising-and-falling wail. "Oh, *blast* it." She glanced at her diamond wrist-watch. "Now I'm going to be late and I'm supposed to be meeting Tim Susskind at the Savoy—I suppose there won't be a taxi for love nor money—I'll never make it—"

"No."

"*Good*bye—" Joyce pronounced this word *Coo*-bahy, an upper-class affectation acquired at the finishing school which had conducted her into the right circles to meet, and subsequently marry, Sir Walter Prescott-Smith. Her accent, and particularly the use of this word, was a source of mildly satirical amusement to her siblings.

"'Bye, Joyce. Be seeing you!"

Joyce hurried off, waving her arm energetically at a possible taxi, the poodle yapping hysterically alongside, while Mado walked home smiling, swinging her string bag.

Indoors, it was already dark. She turned on the kitchen light, hastily pulled down the blackout blind, put away her shopping, and began washing the breakfast dishes.

"Who is it?" said a voice.

"Hullo, Andy. It's me, Mado. How are things?"

"All right." Mado imagined him sitting on the table, as Matt had. "Are the others coming in?"

"Tom will be in by and by. He has some sixth-form thing. Matt's at a lecture."

"Good day at the office?"

"So-so. My secretary had had a bomb and went home early, so I had most of her work to do. Did you have a good day?"

"I went down to look at the Braques at the Tate. And then took in a lunchtime concert at the National Gallery."

"Good programme?"

"I find it hard to concentrate nowadays. Unless something is really outstanding I find my mind beginning to drift back in this direction. Worried about you three, maybe. It's quite a wrench to keep away. But the Braques were worth seeing. I like his green."

"Greener than any grass," Mado agreed.

"Then I looked at paintings by war artists. Dreadful, all blood and munitions. I could do better myself."

"I'm sure you could," she said affectionately. "Why don't you try?"

"Through a medium?"

"Through two mediums, I suppose," she said laughing. "Ah, here's Tom. I'm going to take a bath. But then I want to do lots of ironing—it's nice to have someone to chat to—don't go away—"

In the bath—hot water, this day was coming up to ten plus—she thought lazily about Joyce. Unhealthy, what nonsense. How would Joyce, she wondered, react to Andy. Badly, no doubt.

Later, when she was ironing, she said to Andy, "My elder sister Joyce thinks that Matt and I ought to get married."

"Why don't you?"

"Haven't seen the person I could fancy. Or he hasn't seen me. He's probably off at the war, whoever he is."

"I wouldn't mind marrying you," Andy said thoughtfully.

"Thank you! But you probably wouldn't have when you were—were in your prime. In the days when you knew Topsy."

"Ah, no. My taste then was for something blonde and giggly."

Tom was practising Bach two-part inventions in the next room. "He is improving all the time," said Andy. "He must have an excellent teacher."

"I know. That's why—ah, here's Matt, that's good. My pie will be done in five minutes. Andy, be a love and tell Tom he must stop playing and lay the table for supper."

The siren had just gone, and as Matt came in, they heard the mumble of German bombers overhead. Matt was carrying an ugly fat black cat.

"Good grief!" said his sister. "Where did you pick *her* up?"

"On the stairs. This is no time for her to be out. Her kittens would all have birthmarks."

"Well she can stay the night, but she must leave in the morning. Yes, it's you I'm talking to! In the meantime you can answer to the name of Martha. And I suppose you'll want a bit of pie. One square inch of Spam."

After the meal, Mado read her reports, Matt and Tom played chess, with Andy sometimes suggesting moves for Tom. The black cat settled down by the fire. At one point she stuck out her chin, ecstatically, purring, and they heard Andy's chuckle.

"Are you scratching her chin?"

"She seems to think so."

"I ran into old Coo-bahy," Mado said, mending a pair of socks.

"What was she doing?"

"Getting a taxi to the Savoy. She thinks Tom should be evacuated."

"Just let her try."

Presently Matt had to go off to work. By now the night was punctuated by the steady buzz and drone of the bombers, crackle of anti-aircraft fire, and the regular concussion of bombs falling, but not very near.

"Sounds like the docks again," said Mado. "But do take care, Matt."

"No worry unless there's one with your name written . . . Coo-bahy, then—"

"*Coo*-bahy," they said.

"I ought to go to bed," Mado remarked, after he had gone. But, in spite of that, she stayed on, and the three remaining sat in friendly silence, in the dim warm room.

A week later, the sisters chanced to meet again, standing in a queue for shoes, in Knightsbridge, at half-past eight in the morning.

London was like that in those days, acquaintances kept meeting in odd places.

"Good heavens, Joyce, I'd never have expected to see you up so early."

Joyce looked disgusted with her surroundings.

"My hairdresser told me Abbotts were getting in some red casuals."

"My chemist told *me*."

"Wonder what time they'll open." Joyce shrank deeper into her mink as the line stood patiently, half-visible in the icy fog.

"Half-past nine, perhaps . . . Where's your dog?"

"Left him with our char."

"Lucky to have one. I suppose you wouldn't like a cat?"

"Certainly not! Specially any cat coming from you. Has fleas, probably."

"Almost certainly. But a nice nature. Andy and Tom are fond of her."

"Who *is* this Andy you keep referring to?" said Joyce alertly.

"I told you. Our lodger. Our ghost."

"*Ghost?*"

In the murky, frosty light of daybreak the whole line of hopeful shoe-seekers resembled a procession of grey and dripping ghosts. Joyce directed a baleful glare at her younger sister, whose hair was wound in a roll on a piece of string, and who wore a navy duffel coat spangled with dewdrops.

"How can you talk such balderdash? How do you mean, ghost?"

"Well, he is a ghost," said Mado reasonably. "He used to live in the house, back in the nineties, before it was made into flats. He was a poet, a failure. Wrote one rather quotable piece that's in books of Victorian verse—'If I were King of Nowhere, and you were Queen of Time,' it begins. You must know it. But he knew he was a failure and in the end he gassed himself. Oddly enough, he was a friend of our great-aunt Topsy—knew her quite well, he says—that ought to make him a suitable friend for us, in *your* book—"

"Will you *please* stop talking such utter nonsense!" hissed Joyce, looking nervously up and down the damp and patient queue, as if she expected them to fall on her sister and lynch her. "It's not at all funny and I'm not in the mood for fantasy. *What would Nanny say?*"

Mado waited a moment before replying, and then said gently, "Nanny's dead, as you may recall."

"It's high time you moved out of that place. What an atmosphere for Tom to grow up in. Walter says—"

"Tom seems happy enough. We're all marking time, really, aren't we?" Mado added mildly. "Oh, look, they are starting to open the shop."

But it turned out that there were only shoes enough for twenty customers. The woman in front of Joyce got the last pair.

Thursday was Matt's evening off, so it happened that they were all in the flat together when the land-mine demolished it, reducing the whole building to a heap of smoking rubble.

Wardens and rescue workers got there too late to save the people buried underneath. But a cat escaped, mewing sadly, and an auxiliary fireman, plying his stirrup pump on the dying flames, heard a man's voice calling, "Mado? Matt? Tom? You there? Where are you?"

"*Who's that?* Someone alive in there?" said the AFS man sharply.

But there was no reply, except for a faint murmur of "*Coo*-bahy."

They Have Found Out

Mr Caspy was having a good time buying a ball-point pen in Woolworths. A clipboard with paper attached lay chained to the counter, and Mr Caspy tried quite a number of pens before fixing on the one that seemed best; it did not do to take one that yielded up its ink too freely, or it would run out too soon. He liked to get good value out of his pens, and became extremely annoyed if one of them ran dry under its allotted span of two to three years of use. He always wrapped a tiny jam-pot label, with the date, around the pen as soon as he got home, so that he might know what to expect. And if it expired prematurely he took it back with a complaint. In the same way he marked his marmalade, whisky, apple juice, and milk, so that due measure could be kept on consumption, no commodity used up too fast, or too slowly. (That anything should be consumed too slowly was, of course, not at all a frequent occurrence.) In the same manner margarine, cheese, and bread were marked by faint knife-lines, indicating the day's, or the meal's, portion. Mr Caspy had grown up in World War II, when almost every commodity was rationed; the methodical and orderly habits thus engendered in him had never been relinquished.

Having finally selected his pen, Mr Caspy carefully surveyed Woolworths, a haven to which he paid regular visits, calculating that the cost of the bus ride was well balanced by the savings on articles bought there. He enjoyed, as well, the dazzling light, the warmth, all free, the slightly gritty feel of the narrow-planked floor underfoot—as if glass powder had been sprinkled over it—the perfumed air, redolent with bath essences and inexpensive make-up, the bright colours, the shine and spangle of tin and tinsel, and the confidence engendered by the fact that every article on sale had its price clearly displayed. There was never any need to ask, and be betrayed, by embarrassment, into an unnecessary purchase. Mr Caspy hated asking the price and had more than once forgone some desired object rather than make an inquiry about it. He had a nervous dislike of admitting to ignorance, which had often stood him in bad stead.

Now, having come to the conclusion that nothing else in the shop was, at that juncture, necessary to him, he carefully tore off the strip of paper on which he had tried out the ball-points, rolled it, and tucked it into his jacket pocket. Why make a present of his handwriting to some stranger?

Turning into Smith's the stationers he bought adhesive tape, string, and a small telephone note pad, all of which he knew to be on sale cheaper here than in Woolworths. (The Woolworth pad, at first sight, *appeared* to be a better bargain, but in fact had fewer pages; the tape and string were both longer at Smith's.)

Then, satisfied, he caught his home-bound bus, proffering a return-half ticket which had, of course, been bought at half-price on his Senior Citizen card.

There was a calm pleasure in the slow progress of the bus; while many passengers fidgeted or tapped their feet impatiently at red lights and blocked traffic in congested streets, and then at slow meanderings in the open country and along little-used roads in order to take in the maximum number of rural stops, Mr Caspy merely thought complacently what a lot of mileage he was getting for his money, and how very much this ride would have cost had he been so reckless as to take a taxi. In fact as the bus jolted along he fell asleep, and had a brief but vivid dream: he was seated on a hard bench in the Tuileries Gardens, and was observing a sparrow, with something in its beak, which was being energetically pursued by a gang of other sparrows. It zoomed across the space in front of him, at last dropping its treasure, which proved to be no more than a used yellow Metro ticket. Emily, beside him on the seat, did not think this as funny as he did. She was saying, "Can't we go and have some lunch, dear? I'm awfully hungry—and, after all, we *are* in Paris—it does seem a shame—" and he was saying, "No, no, you'll appreciate your dinner all the more if you work up a good appetite for it."

Mr Caspy woke up as the bus jolted to yet another halt, glanced at his watch, and was pleasantly surprised. His time was insufficiently occupied on the best of days; this inching progress would most handily dispose of the bald, empty space between two and four, quite the worst part of the day. At four it would be permissible to put on a kettle and make tea, saving the tea-bag for future use; at five some acquaintance might telephone, and Mr Caspy could also go out to feel his washed socks on the spindle in the back garden to see if they were dry; at six there was BBC news, most respectably occupying thirty minutes; and, after that, the careful, meticulous preparation of a frugal evening meal permitted another hour, at least, to slip by; then the meal could be slowly consumed, washed down by a medicinal glass of whisky on doctor's orders; then television or radio, eked out by the remains of the morning's newspaper, supplied a satisfactory bridge leading from supper to his solitary bedtime. Mornings were much better. They had an impetus of their own, supplied by the daily harvest of mail, mostly, these days, bills, catalogues and bank statements, but still, something had to be done about them, they could not be allowed to lie dustily or mount up; there was also the newspaper and the need to purchase food and household articles.

It was life; it passed.

Whisky, thought Mr Caspy, in annoyance; he should have bought a bottle at the big cut-price store next to Woolworths; how could he have forgotten? There remained in his current bottle only enough for another eight-and-a-half days.

He took out the new ball-point and made a memorandum in the tiny notebook he carried always in his jacket pocket. Out, at the same time, came the tiny rolled slip of paper on which he had tried the pens; with a touch of bewilderment he read his own writing:

"*They have found out and are coming to get you.*"

What nonsensical impulse had sent those words into his head? What was their origin? Where could he have read, or heard them? On television? *Who* have found out? Found out *what*?

Flushing with exasperation, stuffing the tiny roll of paper back into his pocket, Mr Caspy glanced at the last page of his notebook and was reminded that, after leaving the bus and before going back to his house, he had an appointment at the local doctor's surgery to receive the result of a routine check-up.

One should make the most possible use of the National Health Service, Mr Caspy believed; after all, it's our money that pays those blighters.

Minutes later he was sitting on the hard velvet bench, staring out with impatience at the little fountain that played to itself in the clinic courtyard. What do they need *that* for? he grumbled to himself. It was a total waste of electric current, all coming out of the tax-payers' pocket, mere ridiculous decoration and titivation. However, disciplining himself to ignore the frivolous play of water, Mr Caspy picked up a leaflet on the subject of *Cystitis and You*; after all, one ought to benefit from the free literature they left lavishly lying around.

A bell rang, and he jumped uncontrollably; really they ought to adopt some more civilised, some more dignified, means of summoning patients to the doctors' offices. Patients were not slaves, after all!

"I'm afraid it's not good news, Ted," said Dr Owens. "Though not, perhaps, entirely unexpected?"

Mr Caspy stared, as if, to him, the news was not only unexpected, but wholly, outrageously incredible, invented as a piece of monstrous tomfoolery, some demonic practical joke . . . Meanwhile the doctor went on talking.

"How long is it since Emily died? Fifteen years? Well—" the doctor spread his hands, as if to indicate, we none of us live for ever, do we, and you are a good age after all.

"But *she* died of anaemia—nothing to do with heart—" objected Mr Caspy in a tone full of resentment. He stood up, and gave the doctor's cell-like office a sour scrutiny, as if in search of some appliance which he could not see there.

"Well," said the doctor again, "think over the choices I have given you, and we'll discuss them again in a few days. I don't think—"

What the doctor did not think, Mr Caspy did not wait to hear. He had already turned, angrily snatching up his plastic carrier bag with the string, adhesive tape and telephone pad—string! A whole large new ball of green, glistening string, guaranteed good for outdoor as well as indoor use! And a memo pad at least half an inch thick! Two hundred pages . . .

Proceeding more slowly than was his habit along the quarter-mile walk from the clinic to his cottage, Mr Caspy observed three temporary road signs—red-bordered white triangles, set up along the grass verge to alert motorists:

SLOW—TOADS CROSSING

They make motorists slow down for toads, thought Mr Caspy morosely, but not for pedestrians, oh no. At present there were no indications of toads; perhaps they preferred to perform their crossing at night. Where were they travelling *to*? Why did toads wish to get to the other side of the road? What happened to them there?

Did they ever go back?

Arrived at his own gate, Mr Caspy saw with annoyance that some person had been through the gate and had left the metal hasp thrown back, not hooked over the gatepost. The postman probably, stupid, careless indifferent fellow. If a wind had blown up, there was only a frail, ancient latch to hold the heavy wooden gate; it might easily have blown open, slammed and swung all afternoon, knocked the whole gate right off its hinges. And the gravel path needed raking again, gravel was all scuffed to the side, tufts of grass growing in the middle and dead leaves, slippery, dangerous. He must speak to Jim Ward, tell him to rake it. But who for?

Scraping his shoes carefully on the metal grid by the door—one *paid* for the gravel, after all, no sense in carrying it indoors—Mr Caspy turned his key and entered the dark house.

Of course it was not really dark, only dusk, and he walked into what—since Emily died—he had thought of as his den. It faced west, catching the warm honey-coloured light of the setting sun, and was, especially at this time of day, his favourite spot in the house. An old red Turkey carpet, acquired second-hand at a hotel sale, covered the floor; a leather-covered couch and armchair, much worn but comfortable, and a battered roll-top desk, crammed with dusty papers, made the room indisputably his, a male domain; Emily's leather-framed photograph on the desk seemed present on sufferance, like the token female member of a committee, existing to prove lack of prejudice.

With an exclamation of annoyance Mr Caspy moved to right the photograph which for some mysterious reason had fallen on to its face. Could there have been a mild earthquake? Or—conceivably—burglars? But no, all else seemed undisturbed.

Then, glancing round him, Mr Caspy let out a second gasp—of disgust this time. For, all over the dark-red carpet, where oblongs of late sun revealed the worn, dusty condition of the pile—Mr Caspy now saw the silvery tracks of snails—or slugs—crossing and recrossing the warp. Hundreds and hundreds of them!

Dropping the bag on his untidy desk, he hurried back to the kitchen for the vacuum cleaner, assembled its component parts, plugged it into the socket under the desk (a most inconvenient location) and proceeded to give the carpet a vigorous going-over, muttering, "Horrible—foul—revolting," as he worked. "How could they have got into the house? Where are they now? There must have been a hundred of them," he said again.

The cleaner flashed its red light, indicating that the dustbag needed emptying, and Mr Caspy almost snarled with annoyance. This was his least favourite of all household tasks, and the evening was drawing in, soon it would be time for the BBC news and his glass of whisky. But things must be done properly and in order: he switched off the cleaner and pressed the bakelite catch to release the lid at the end of the barrel-shaped body. The dustbag was certainly full to overflowing with packed, grey, gritty, hairy dust—the very last object ingested being a tiny furry roll of paper.

Mr Caspy unrolled it and read again the words, "*They have found out and are coming to get you*", in his own handwriting.

With a snort of impatience, he poked it back into the dustbag and carried the whole thing out to the dustbin behind the back door, where, by the porch light, he began the careful, distasteful task of sorting through every handful of dust before consigning it to the bin. One never knew what might get accidentally sucked up; vacuum cleaners were far too powerful these days, quite unnecessarily so. There! A penny! When he was young no cleaner could have sucked that up. And half a dozen large bits of gravel, which he carefully returned to the path. Gravel costs money. And the top of a pen—that might come in useful. But to whom? Indignantly, as he avoided some shards of broken glass, Mr Caspy reviewed the contents of his house: the half rolls of toilet paper in both lavatories, the almost new cakes of soap—the towels—the good pair of new walking boots. The four inches of whisky.

Turning, with the emptied bag in his gritty hands, he saw, illuminated by the porch light, a procession of toads hopping one by one through the back door.

"Aaaaargh!" screamed Mr Caspy. "Just *wait* till I get after you!" and he rushed past them to re-assemble the vacuum cleaner. "Just *wait* till I get at you!" he shouted again furiously, scrubbing with his jacket sleeve at the beads of sweat that rolled down his brow and cheeks.

Three days later Mr Caspy was discovered by the indifferent postman who, thinking it odd that the backdoor had stood open on all his last visits, stepped inside and found the householder lying on top of his vacuum cleaner. It was concluded by the coroner that Mr Caspy must have given himself a lethal shock in pulling out the plug; considering the state of his heart, the doctor said, quite a mild shock would have been sufficient to carry him off.

No toads were seen. Presumably they had proceeded to their onward destination. But Mr Caspy had been rather disagreeably nibbled by slugs.

A Rhyme for Silver

Eighteen-year-old Jeff Tichborne worked in Goodman's TV and Radio Repair department. His younger brother Simon always enjoyed passing the shop window, which was brilliantly lit and packed with television screens, curved coloured glass rectangles, each showing a different picture of distant places all over the globe and what was going on there—football matches, volcanoes erupting, yachts capsising, people planting rice, waterfalls, great bulldozers chewing away at the desert.

"It's like a live atlas," Simon said contentedly, leaning back in the wheelchair as Aunt Gwen pushed him homewards. She took Simon to the clinic three days a week: what was done to him there didn't seem to help, in fact it made him feel worse, but they said it was for his benefit so he supposed he must put up with it good-temperedly. In the end it would make little difference, but perhaps by then they would have learned facts that would help other people.

Simon lay back, consciously relaxing to quell the choked feeling that arose from treatment at the clinic, and looking forward to the evening. Evenings never varied: Jeff read aloud —poetry, his own or other people's—and if there was a travel film on TV they looked at it.

Simon was small and dark-haired and very calm; he liked to laugh too, and found a lot of things surprisingly funny, but few people knew that, apart from Jeff and Aunt Gwen. Simon worried sometimes about Jeff, but kept the worry to himself: only the future could untie *that* knot.

Jeff came home at six in a bad temper.

"Old Goodman says I take too long on repair jobs, doing them too carefully," he growled, shovelling down hamburger and chips. "*He* says it doesn't pay off—all I need do is just join two ends together."

Simon watched his skinny, active, red-haired brother nostalgically. Once he too could have eaten hamburger and chips, but not any more; thin soup or milk was his lot now, day in day out.

"You mustn't go against Mr Goodman, Jeffie," said Aunt Gwen, all of a twitter. She was a pale wispy woman with hair in a shiny net. "Not the way things are, with—with the rent rise and prices going up all the time. You have to do the job his way."

"I know, I know," said Jeff, slamming tea into his mug. Jeff's earnings had supported the family since Mr and Mrs Tichborne had been killed in a coach crash on the M5 two years ago. His college plans had to be put off, perhaps permanently, for Aunt Gwen's time was mainly spent on looking after Simon, and would be even more, quite soon.

"Goodman's full of slime—he's like an overripe puffball. One minute smarming the customers, next minute telling me to skimp on the job. And then he'll ask after Sim in that oozy sugary voice: 'How's the little fellow getting on? Is he any better?' Ugh! he makes me sick!"

"What's your parrot's name?" said Sim softly, and Jeff burst into an unwilling guffaw, remembering the time last summer when Mr Goodman had come with the truck to pick him up for an emergency repair. There had been an owl on the draining-board: Jeff had found it, stunned, in Dyeworks Lane the previous evening, and Sim, who loved wild creatures and was clever with them, had dressed a wound on its wing and given it brandy. Two days later it was well enough to fly away, but in the meantime Mr Goodman, calling, had mistaken it for a parrot.

"He asked after the parrot, just last week. I said it had flown away."

"What did he say?"

"Oh, what a shame. The little fellow ought to have a pet."

"A nice fluffy kitten with a blue ribbon," suggested Sim.

Then they watched a film about the Amazon, and, after it finished, Jeff read aloud his latest which was called 'Group Therapy', and Sim made some useful criticisms. Then, as he often did, Sim asked for Chidiock Tichborne's poem, and Jeff read that.

Next Sunday afternoon Sim was out in the front garden in his wheelchair, making a careful drawing of Mrs Trevor's Labrador, Sootie, who lay heaving in the sun on the next-door lawn, when Mr Goodman drove up in the truck to collect Jeff for another urgent repair job.

"That's right, that's right," he said, giving Sim's drawing an indulgent glance. "Pretty good, eh?" Sim drew formidably well. "I suppose you'd like a doggie of your own, wouldn't you? What's your favourite sort?"

"No—I don't want a dog." Foreseeing all kinds of tiresomeness if Mr Goodman took this notion into his head, Sim added quickly and absently, "I'd rather take a trip to Niagara." On the grass beside him lay a library book which contained six different painters' views of the waterfall; Sim had been thinking how very nice it would be to paint his own version, and add a seventh to the total. *That* would be a thing to leave behind. Sim knew that he was due to die, not very far in the future; he had grown accustomed to the prospect and didn't particularly mind it, but there were things he wanted to do first.

"A trip to Niagara? Well I never!" said Mr Goodman, quite taken aback. For the moment he was silenced. Later in the week, though, he told Jeff, "You ought to get your younger brother to Niagara if that's what he wants. After all, there isn't much—" He thought for a moment and added, "Maybe the local paper would do an appeal."

Jeff scowled without answering. He loathed the idea of charity.

"Do you really want to see Niagara so badly?" he asked Simon that evening.

"No, no; old Goodman got carried away by sentiment as usual." Just the same, he had a distant look in his eye that troubled his brother.

Jeff had read stories in the paper about dying children who longed to go to a Butlins camp or Buckingham Palace or Southend, and kind neighbours who clubbed together to arrange the treat. He found the idea a bit sickening. Fine for the neighbours who, no doubt, felt all puffed up with virtue and kindness. But what about the children, after the treat was over, when all they had was death to wait for? Had they really been done such a good turn?

Sim was different, of course: Sim was special. He had done such a lot of thinking in his life that in some ways he seemed the older of the two brothers.

Niagara, though! That was going to cost a fortune!

Jeff began thinking about ways of earning money. Then he saw the advertisement in the local paper: GUARD WANTED.

His annual three-week holiday was due. He had intended to spend it moonlighting, freelancing on electrical repair jobs, but that would annoy Mr Goodman very much if he got to hear of it, as he undoubtedly would; and the newspaper offer was not bad pay, eighty pounds a week. Two hundred and forty pounds with what Jeff had saved up . . .

He went and inquired about the job at the office of the local Nature Conservancy Board.

"You realise it would be a non-stop watching responsibility?" said Miss Plowright, the secretary of the Board, who interviewed him. "We have guards alternating in twelve-hour shifts. And you have to stay right there, all the time. Five minutes away from the spot, and somebody could whip in; then all of the work would have been for nothing."

"Yes I do see that," said Jeff, quite trembling with anxiety.

"What's your job—when you aren't doing guard work?" asked Miss Plowright, studying Jeff with curiosity. She thought he looked too thin and too angry, and perhaps too imbued with imagination for his own good—imagination that was never, or hardly ever, allowed out for an airing.

She thought of moles, burrowing in the dark, with their powerful claws: what happens to moles' claws if they are not allowed to burrow?

"I—oh, I'm a poet," said Jeff absently. "I mean I'm an electrician," he added next minute, blushing with fury. He had been thinking how much he was going to enjoy sitting out all night on the grassy hillside, thinking how, for once, he would have *time* to think.

"A poet? Or an electrician?" Miss Plowright smiled slowly. "Nothing to stop you being both."

"Well I had an ancestor who was a poet. At least, he wrote one poem."

Now why had he told the woman that? But she did not seem at all surprised; perhaps people often told her things.

"Tichborne, Tichborne," she murmured. "I know that

name. Didn't he plot against the queen? And write a very sad poem on the eve of his execution?"

"He was a Catholic, you see. He was only twenty-eight when they executed him."

> "My tale was heard, and yet it was not told
> My fruit is fallen, yet my leaves are green—"

"That's the one."

"He is certainly an ancestor to put you on your mettle," said Miss Plowright. "I can see it will be a job to live up to him."

Jeff thought, recklessly, of telling her that they had yet another ancestor, Elspeth Tichborne, accused of witchcraft and burned at the stake, leaving, with her dying breath, such a curse on the judges who condemned her that all three died of the plague the following year. But he did not, and later was glad that he had not.

Miss Plowright was going on thoughtfully, "I can quite see why this kind of job had an appeal for you. What kind of poet are you?" And, as he looked blank, "Traditional or otherwise?"

"Oh, traditional."

"Regular metre? Rhyme?"

"Yes."

"Hmm, that's a pity."

"Why?"

"You might be so occupied trying to think of a rhyme that you would let the thieves get past you."

"I would not!" said Jeff, stung. Later he was to remember that too.

"All right, all right, I trust you!" she said. "And the job's yours. Night shift. I must say I do prefer rhyming poetry myself. Now, I'll tell you where to find the site. Here's a large-scale map. And don't, please, *don't* breathe a word to a single soul, not your nearest and dearest, *nobody*. This job is no joke, you know, it's deadly serious. We aren't paying out a hundred and sixty pounds a week just for fun."

"Not a single soul," promised Jeff, wondering how he was going to explain his night-time activities to Sim and Aunt Gwen.

But Miss Plowright said, "Of course, you can tell them that you are guarding a plant. But not just what and where. Or—seriously—you might be followed."

"It's like a spy story."

"It's almost worse. The things that selfish, greedy, uncaring people will do for money: or for rare specimens. In spite of the fact that there would be a fine of a thousand pounds for each plant stolen—very likely a prison sentence too. It's an endangered species, you see; there are only two known sites where it grows in England. Sad, really: when your ancestor wrote his poem there might have been hundreds of them, scattered all over the Downs. But, with ploughing, and herbicides and ignorant people who pick them—"

"And greedy, *un*-ignorant people who dig them up—"

"Yes, and of course they are also subject to the ordinary risks that affect any plant—they may be trodden on by cows, or nibbled by rabbits or flattened by motorbike scramblers . . . Well, there you have it. Enjoy your watching. Recite your ancestor's poem, if you can't think up one of your own, and *keep awake*."

Mr Goodman dropped in, one evening during Jeff's three-week leave.

"I know the lad's on holiday, but I thought as I knew he

wasn't going away . . . and I reckoned he'd be pleased to pick up a bit of extra cash—"

It was another urgent repair job.

"I'm afraid my nephew's not here," said Aunt Gwen, flustered.

"Ah? Out enjoying himself, is he? Don't blame him."

Sim thought dispassionately that Mr Goodman's round pink face, with the little deep-sunk eyes like sparks, was like a fruit that has begun to decay, a soggy tomato with the stem sinking into a tiny wrinkled pit, and the flesh under the skin turning soft and rotten. For some obscure reason the look of it recalled great-great-great-grandmother Elspeth's curse: "I curse the lips that spake the sentence and the hard hearts that ordained it; I curse the hands that writ the accusation and the bodies that bore them; may they rot before the grave, and die before death take them, and roast in hell-fire eternally thereafter . . ."

"No—no, he's out on a job," twittered Aunt Gwen. "To earn enough to send Simmie here away on a trip—"

Sim heaved a resigned sigh.

Mr Goodman said, "Niagara! yes, yes of course! And a grand sight it'll be, young man, when you get there, it will indeed. Repair job?" probed Mr Goodman sharply and delicately. "Not going behind my back to any of my customers, I hope?"

"No, no, of course not, not a repair job. Watching over a plant—"

Sim looked gravely at Aunt Gwen, who bit her lip and shut up. But Mr Goodman went right on probing.

"A plant, eh? That's interesting! One of those rare ones the World Wildlife folk are so hot on preserving? Funny, isn't it, really, they should spend so much on that when there's so much money wanted for other things—research on illness—

like the lad here, and people dying of starvation in Africa and all the homeless . . . Mind you, I'm keen on plants meself, got a nice few lilies and tropical orchids in my little greenhouse, they've no better specimens at Kew though I do say so—but you've got to have a sense of proportion, haven't you? Would it be an orchid, then, the boy's minding?"

"I can't say," said Aunt Gwen faintly. "He never told us."

"Very right, very right. Very right. Can't trust anybody, these days. Maybe it'd be one of those monkey orchids, it's said they grow round here, up on Tillingham Down. *Very* uncommon, those are—there's a few more over in Berkshire, and that's all they know of. You'd like to see them, I daresay, wouldn't you, young man? You could make one of your drawings of them, maybe?"

"I'm not very good at drawing plants," Sim said politely.

"No? Well, I mustn't stand here with the grass growing under my feet . . ."

Mr Goodman trotted out, his pink face shining, paused for a word with Mrs Trevor in her garden next door, who nodded and pointed to the right; then he shot off in his repair truck with the electric flashes in gold and green and Goodman's Lightning Service blazoned along the side.

The first week passed quickly, and the second.

There was, of course, an easy way up on to Tillingham Down: first the road until you came to Gamekeeper's Cottages, then across a farmyard past three silos, along by a wheatfield and up a chalk track beside a beechwood. But, in order to foil possible observers, Jeff and his co-watcher, a dour chemistry student called Pat Jones from Leeds, adopted various roundabout routes to the site, scrambling up the side of the hill through the steep hanging woods, or right round to the back and across the racecourse, or up the Roman road two miles away eastwards and so along the top of the ridge. Jeff began to know the little patch of woodland and the clearing where the orchid grew as well as his own front garden.

And the flowers? They were strange little twisted knots at the top of pale three-inch stems, tiny things, too unimportant-looking to be deemed worthy of so much care and surveillance. They were withered, the flowering-time was past—that was in May of course—and seed-pods were already forming; but Miss Plowright had shown Jeff pictures, and then he had looked them up himself at home in the *Concise British Flora.* They were a purplish, reddish colour, had two tiny legs, two tiny arms, a tail, a head with an infinitesimal darkish face—malevolent—two dots of green eyes and a kind of bishop's mitre, three-pointed, in a lighter pink matching the pale pink stomach. A monkey bishop! Strangely enough, the little monkey-faces in the picture had a definite look of young Sim—there was something of his perky, detached quality in the way they stood springily on their stalks.

Jeff had grown to be very fond of them; he had a fatherly, protective attitude towards the withered little entities, waiting so mildly for their seed-time and the end of summer. Here they had grown, here they waited, in this same hollow of downland, perhaps for hundreds of years, while kings came to the throne and went, while wars were fought, while Chidiock Tichborne wrote his poem and waited for the executioner, while great-great-great-grandmother reviled the bishops and judges, swore that she was innocent of the charges they laid against her and then went up in flames.

Why are people so horrible to each other? Jeff wondered, sitting in the quiet dewy woods which were never completely silent at night, and never quite dark. The sky, crammed with stars, hung low over the trees; then, long before sunrise, the stars faded and the sky brightened. Always, somewhere, there was something in motion—a twig snapping or a fan of leaves rustling. At first Jeff was nervous of these noises, expected wolves or bandits or boa constrictors, he hardly knew what. But soon he became accustomed to the sounds: they were just the night creatures of the woods, going about their business.

But why *are* people so horrible? They were no worse, those people in bygone days, than we are now. We are no more civilised than they were, we shoot and fight each other on the least excuse, we grab and steal what is not ours. Take the people who are after this little orchid. Why can't they leave it to grow in peace? How can somebody who has enough specialised knowledge to be aware of its value still be so callously selfish? You'd think that orchid hunters would be a cut above other collectors, but no, they are just as greedy and ruthless, just as ready to break laws and do irreparable damage.

A plaguing mischief light on ye, hateful brigands! Elspeth Tichborne had shouted, as they tied her to the stake. My curse on the lot of ye! May the sun never warm ye, nor water quench your thirst. May the seeds shrivel that ye plant, and the food turn to gall in your bellies. I am innocent, and shall declare it to the last.

But they had burned her just the same.

In the third week, Sim caught a cold. This was serious, for Sim had no resistance at all to germs, any bacillus that floated by could knock him endways. From germs at the clinic, of course, it was impossible to protect him, and Jeff privately thought that the clinic was the source of many of their problems; but this time it was indubitably Mr Goodman, who dropped in one teatime to inquire if Jeff would be free to come and rewire a church hall that evening.

"What? Still going off on those late-night outings? *We* know what to think when a young feller is out all night for weeks on end, don't we, Miss Tichborne?" With a wink. "Oh, I know, I know, he says he's watching over the monkey orchid —but we know better than that, don't we?"

"I never said anything about what I was doing," corrected Jeff.

"Nor you did! Nor you did. Just me going on. Why, if you were doing that, you'd not have to worry about raising cash to send the laddie to Niagara. They say there's collectors who'd pay thousands for a single seed-pod."

Mr Goodman fixed Jeff with an eye like a laser beam.

"Of *course* an honest young feller-me-lad like you, that does his work so carefully, would never pay any heed to types like that. HECK-tishoooooo!" He gave a tremendous sneeze. "Got a bit of a cold, been out late too many nights meself—doing your work for you, young Jeff."

Squawking remonstrance, Aunt Gwen almost pushed Mr Goodman out of the kitchen. But the mischief was done: next day Sim was reduced to a limp flop of gasping misery, needed non-stop nursing and an oxygen cylinder in his room.

It was after three days of this, helping Aunt Gwen nurse by day, watching by night, that Jeff one night fell asleep under his hawthorn spinney, while trying to think of a rhyme for silver.

When he awoke, in the dripping hush of a grey and sodden dawn, the seed heads were gone. The monkey orchid stems had been clipped, very neatly, with scissors, close to the base.

For about ten minutes Jeff was numb with shock. He sat staring at the patch of ground: he literally found it impossible to believe his eyes. But there were the thirteen raw little stumps, and a couple of dark, bruised footprints in the rain-soaked turf. He found a crushed hollow in a nearby bramble-clump, where somebody had stood and waited. Jeff detested the thought of that, almost more than all else: that a person, his enemy, had stood there, watching, studying him, perhaps for several nights, waiting to pounce on the single moment of oblivion. And at last it had come. And Jeff had failed in his task. And the seed heads were gone.

"They weren't even mature," mourned Miss Plowright. "They weren't ripe, and now the seeds won't germinate. He won't get any good out of them—whoever he is."

"I didn't tell anybody. I never even said the name." Jeff wished he were dead and underground. Miss Plowright looked at him sadly. He couldn't bear the look in her eyes. Perhaps she believed he had taken them? Had sold them?

"I'm sure you didn't," she said. "The fact that someone knew where they were need not be your fault at all. These things get around."

"It's my fault they were stolen," said Jeff. "*I* fell asleep." Wretchedly he stared back at Miss Plowright, with eyes full of tears. And she had no comfort to offer him.

"She did offer me the pay, but of course I wouldn't take it," he told Aunt Gwen later.

"*Course* you couldn't," croaked Sim, who, mercifully, was a little better that morning, off the oxygen and even able to drink some orange juice from a cup.

Then Sim added thoughtfully, "I'm going to put great-great-great-grandma's curse on whoever took the monkey orchid. Maybe that'll protect all the other specimens, too."

"Don't try to talk, child, you'll tire yourself," warned Aunt Gwen, carrying a bowl and towel out of the room. But Jeff could see that the idea of the curse was a distraction from his own misery and discomfort.

Sim went on slowly, "I bet if great-granny Elspeth had

been in charge of the orchids, she'd have set a guardian by them."

"What sort of guardian?" asked Jeff, humouring him.

"Like a great black shaggy monkey—but shapeless and soggy, with cold arms, ice-cold hands and feet that would grab you and hold you tight to its soggy chest. And it would puff into your face with its cold stinking breath—like the smell from a dustbin. It would feel like all the hate in the world, come to grab you: hate that's been piling up for hundreds of years."

"Don't!" said Jeff with a shiver. Sim's words somehow embodied the very thought he had had in his own mind; he could feel the awful black thing take shape and expand, like a heaving black balloon, out there, or in there—

To distract himself from the thought he said, "I'm sorry, I'm really sorry about Niagara, Simmie."

"Oh, that's all right. Niagara doesn't matter a bit," Sim said absently. "I don't suppose I'd have been able to draw it, anyway. Why don't you collect me a lot of those beer-can tops, the ones with loops and rings? I've got an awfully good idea for making a pattern."

Mr Goodman was extremely shocked when he heard, after Jeff had gone back to work, that the two hundred and forty pounds had not been paid and the Niagara trip was off.

"No! Well I never! What a blessed shame! I'm *surprised* at those people. After all, you did the watching, quite OK, for two and a half weeks, you ought to have been paid for *that.* They might at least have paid you two hundred—or two-twenty." He seemed really outraged, and paid no heed when Jeff said he wouldn't have accepted the money anyway. "I hate for that poor mite of a lad to be disappointed, when he's got nothing else to look forward to."

Mr Goodman worked for a while in silence, sorting invoices. He seemed to be turning Sim's condition over in his mind, perhaps comparing it to his own—today, for some reason, he seemed particularly pink and pleased with himself. He said, "Business isn't bad, I've had one or two strokes of luck lately, maybe I could see my way to a bit of a donation—"

Jeff stared at him in horror. He muttered, "Oh, no, that wouldn't—" and then found he couldn't bear to stay in Mr Goodman's presence a moment longer. There was something about those pink cheeks, those bright little eyes, those big clever fingers so handy with pliers or screwdriver, that made him feel sick. He bolted out saying something about a thermostat.

But late that evening, when Jeff arrived home through thundery rain, he found Mr Goodman there already with Aunt Gwen, making his offer. "I'll be only too glad to pay the lad's fare, if that's what he's set his heart on. In fact I've a cheque already written—"

"But it's not what I've set my heart on, Mr Goodman," whispered Sim. "I don't feel quite up to drawing Niagara. Instead I'm planning a picture of my great-great-great-grandmother's curse. D'you want to hear about it, Mr Goodman? She put it on the people who did her harm. It looks like a gathering—a great poisoned swelling in the shape of a monkey that will grow inside a person, inside the thief who stole the flowers that Jeff was looking after. Soon, very soon, it will burst out of that person, like a seed out of a pod—"

"*Don't* Sim!" cried out Jeff. "You mustn't!"

But Mr Goodman, without waiting for Sim to finish, had run out of the room and out of the house. A jag of lightning greeted him, and a flurry of rain: summer was breaking up fast.

"What in the world ails the man?" demanded Aunt Gwen, coming in with a cup of milk. "Was he taken ill? He looked terrible."

"He's afraid of illness," Sim said calmly. "Did you remember to bring me any beer-can tops, Jeff?"

"I did find half a dozen." Jeff looked dazed. Slowly he emptied his pockets. "Here . . ." He was thinking about the monkey: the black, wet, heavy, hating monkey. Gradually, by slow degrees, it lifted itself away from him and drifted away, after Mr Goodman, into the outside world. Let it go! Let it never come back! "Here they are," he said, and arranged the can tops on Sim's bedside table.

Sim, still too weak to make a drawing of them, lay back on his pillow and looked them over with great content.

"They'll do nicely," he said.

The two brothers rested in silence until Sim sighed and murmured, "Say Chidiock's poem. Say it all through."

> "My prime of youth is but a frost of cares
> My feast of joy is but a dish of pain
> My crop of corn is but a field of tares
> And all my good is but vain hope of gain.
> The day is past and yet I saw no sun
> And now I live and now my life is done."

Jeff said the other two verses as well.

"It's very good," Sim mumbled. "Listen to how those words plod along, like a slow march. Like a person walking through mud. But you'll write one as good, by and by. Did you finish the one you were working on last night?"

"No. I stuck on a rhyme for silver."

"You'll finish it some time," said Sim.

*

Jeff was out of a job, after Mr Goodman's unexpected death, but Miss Plowright offered him one.

"Would you trust me?" he said.

"Of course I would! I could see how dreadfully upset you were about those seeds. And there are lots of things you can do for us if you care to learn a bit about plants. Perhaps you could go to evening classes."

"I'd like to do that," said Jeff. "Later."

Miss Plowright, who had come to the Tichbornes' house, understood him perfectly.

"Of course, later. I believe your brother is handy with wild creatures? I've got a hedgehog here that was found on the Canterbury road—we've mended its leg, but it needs a place to convalesce for a few days. Do you think—your garden—?"

Sim smiled gently at Miss Plowright. They seemed to have made friends without even having exchanged a single word.

Little Nym

They comes and they goes. And, mainly, there's fewer of 'em goes than comes. That's on account of little Nym. Furriners from outside don't know about little Nym, and nobody living here in the village is liable to tell about him—why should they? You don't go gabbing to folk from other parts about troubles and shames in your own home. And little Nym's was a black shame.

His trouble would be nigh on a hundred years ago now. My dad—and he died ten year ago come Michaelmas, he'd have reached his hundred next August—Dad's older brother Bert was fourteen when the bad thing happened. Uncle Bert remembered it all, plain as the bombers in World War II. And he telled my dad. And Dad telled me. And there's plenty others in the village had it handed down in the same way, quiet-like. But it's not spoken about in the street, nor written down in histories.

'Tis on account of little Nym that, time and again, Hawksmoor Hall comes up for sale on the house agent's list; we'll see that old photo they always puts in the paper, showing the big twisted chimneys and the gabling; *Handsome Period Residence*, it says; and weeds begin to sprout in the drive, and Blishen and Pankhurst's FOR SALE board nailed to the gate. Then a new lot will come, and start all over again.

The house ain't bad; if you've a mind for all that oak panelling and polished floors and great big open fireplaces. (I've sheltered accommodation myself, a nice little flat in the

Penfold Council Estate, with gas heating and wall-to-wall carpet; that suits me right well.) But, summer and winter, I've been in Hawksmoor Hall, many and many a time, and felt nothing unked there. Chimney sweep, I used to be; I reckon I knows all the chimneys for twenty mile round like the palm of me hand; a sweeter set of chimneys you won't find than those at Hawksmoor. (Why *Hawksmoor*, don't ask me; there's no hawks and there's no moor; the house sets in the middle of the village, lying back a furlong or so, behind a birch coppice, so's you don't see it from the road.)

When I give up the chimney sweeping I worked for a spell as painter and plasterer with my cousin Fred Muffett the builder, so I been into Hawksmoor plenty times doing work there; and, like I say, felt no harm in the place.

What I did feel was little Nym; and that was in the garden.

Being as the house has changed hands so often, the new folk coming in always wants summat done, or summat altered; new paint in the big downstairs room that faces southerly towards Tarbury Down, or a new bathroom taken off of one of the first-floor bedrooms, or a kids' playroom fixed up in the attics. There's a rare old rats' ramble of attics up there in the Hall; I reckon little Nym musta slept in one o' them.

Nigh on a dozen times I musta been up there in the house working, painting, plastering over a fireplace for one lot of newcomers, or pulling the plaster off again for the next lot. "Just whatever you say, Marm, yes, it do seem a shame to cover up all that there Tudor brickwork." Or, "Yes, the old ranges musta been right okkerd to manage. Nothing like a nice modern Aga to make a kitchen feel cosy."

And all the days and weeks I worked in the house, on my lone or with others, I never saw nothing nor heard nothing. Bar a few creaks in the joists. And you get those in new buildings, just as often as in old. More, if the truth be told.

But after they've put in their new partitions and fancy cookers and built-in bookshelves and double glazing, the new folk never bide long; sometimes they are out before the daffs have bloomed twice in the garden.

Rare lot of daffs, up at the Hall; I reckon they've been a-growing and a-spreading for over a hundred years. Old Mus' Pettigrew had 'em put in, 'tis said, and the snowdrops too, that grow under the big cedar in the middle of the south lawn; regular carpet they are, come February, if it's been a warm winter. *Lord* Pettigrew, he got to be, by the end; raised up to be a lord, on account of all the poetry he wrote, according to what I heard. And had dinner with the old Queen, and all. He had the garden planned out new, and dunnamany trees planted; but then, after the business of little Nym, they moved away and he built hisself a big house on Telegraph Hill; turned that into a museum, the County Council have now, but I never troubled to go there; I got no time for museums.

Turned jobbing gardener, I done, when I come due for me old age pension and retired from the building trade; that's how I happen to take care of the garden here, two days a week; Blishen and Pankhurst keep me on, even between times, so's the place don't run back too much after folk have moved out.

And that's how I come to have a notion of little Nym.

See him? No, I can't rightly say I done so. But a notion of him, yes, that I do have.

Poor little beggar. He don't mean no harm to me; nor to any soul, rightly, I daresay. Though it do be the young'uns that comes to grief on account of him. Me, he don't take a mite o' notice of; except, once in a while, often of a damp dripply day when the mist lays low over Tarbury Down, the kind of day when there'd be no grown folk about the garden and he could run free; or, when the season's turning, cherry leaves a-reddening, or when the wild hyacinth leaves start to show in the wintry orchard grass; then I'll feel little Nym like a quickness in the air. I'll feel him close by me, or over there, t'other side of the cabbage bed with his head up, sniffing the breeze, keen as a terrier. Mortal full o' questions, he seem to be, at such times: what makes the trees grow? what makes the blue of the sky? why does the earth-worms tug down the birk-leaves under the mould? why do the mouldywarp travel in a straight line, how can he know to do so if he be blind?

All these things little Nym musta wanted an answer to, once, and not a soul about the place troubled to talk to him or take any notice. I can feel his pain, sharp as a sickness, burning and burning.

Ugly, he were, see, poor little sprit: big head, like a balloon, tiny slanting porker's eyes, and big ears that drew out; besides that, a big red marring birthmark as if summun had turned and given him a swipe; he never growed big but was puny with arms and legs no thicker than pea-sticks. And the others: all so big and handsome, the boys, or bright and purty, the gals, never took no notice of him. How do I know that? There's a photo, just one, in the Parish Journal for 1884, showing the May Day Revels: there's the whole family in the garden here, a-watching the crownation of the May Queen. You can see Lord Pettigrew, as he were by then (why they'd turn a chap into a Lord just for writing a whole mess of poems, don't ask; seems a daft-like thing to do;) anyway, there he be, thatch o' white hair, white beard long as a hank of hay, tall and skinny; and there's the rest o' the young'uns, eight altogether, the lads in their nankeens and bum-freezers, the gals in muslins and frilly drawers and sunbonnets; and, peeking out from behind one o' them, this little runt, knee-high to a wanling, with an ugly face and a scared look on it, as if he knowed he shouldn't be there, knowed the others are all sick ashamed of him.

He was the death of his mum, see; she died when he come into the world. Maybe, if she'd not, matters mighta turned out otherways.

'Twas the year after that picture was took that they all flitted to Telegraph Hill.

All but little Nym. He'd died by then.

In them times, o' course, they didn't have no Health Visitors, nor Social Service Workers, nor Probation Officers, nor all the other busybodies that's allowed to come pestering now, knowing your business bettern than their own. Not that it seems to make a heap o' difference, plenty times. Kids get ill done by now just as much, many a striping's handed out, from what you reads in the paper.

Most in gineral it'll be a family that moves into Hawksmoor Hall. 'Family house' it's always billed as; that passel of attics, eight bedrooms, tennis-court and stabling, who'd think of taking it but folk with a mort o' children? And a regiment of servants? And with Tarbury Down just there across the medder, so all the young'uns has to do is scamper over the stile and off, when they want to get away from Dad and Mum, or the governess and under-nursery-maid.

But little Nym couldn't run. He were lame from birth and could only doddle about.

Anyway, as I said, in the main it's big families that take the house. And, time and again, there's been a death. Time out o' mind. Most times it'll be one of the young'uns. And nearly always the littlest. You'd think word woulda passed around by now, would have got to the new buyers, but no; seems there's always a new lot as hasn't heard, happy to put down their cash for a roomy, handsome brick-and-stone house, with a fine well-planted garden, and stables, and all, so close to the Downs.

They lays down their cash, they buys the house and settles in. Next thing, a kid has died. Sometimes 'tis one cause, sometimes another. Croup carried off little Teddy Laleham; young Marcie Mildenhall took the measles very bad and died o' that, with complifications; Annette Blakeney got meningitis and was gone in three days though they whipped her into St Magnus Hospital over to Portsbourne; Thomas Weller had a fall off his pony and died of a busted neck; little Grace Kellaway, the latest of them but one, she just pined away. That's what *I* called it; her mum had a fancy name for it, Anny-rexy Nervosa.

"Oh, Sam," she says to me with tears in her eyes, "try as I will—try as we *all* will—we *cannot* make her eat enough. Can't you try—if we bring her dinner out of doors? She's main fond of you, Sam—please help us!"

It was true, the little thing used to follow me about when I was a-digging or planting-out; I say little, for she looked about seven, though I believe she was going on twelve. They'd moved to the country hoping 'twould help her; but it only made her much worse.

"Won't you eat your nice meat and taties, Gracie?" I'd say to her, as she'd sit on a pile of bricks nigh me in the greenhouse. "There be ice-cream to foller, Mrs Huckley telled me."

"I don't fancy ice-cream, Sam," she'd answer, gulping. "And the meat and taties tastes *horrible*—like garbage that's rotted away, like old slimy cabbage. I can't stand it."

Not enough to keep a wren alive, would she take. O' course I knew the reason for it well enough. But, like I said, we don't mention the tale hereabouts.

I done my best though.

"Marm, you gotta get her away from here," I telled Mrs Kellaway. "This house ain't wholesome for childer."

A nice lady she were, but no manner o' use when it come to argufication. "Get her away where 'tis warm, to France or one o' they furrin lands," I telled her.

"It's no good, Sam," she'd answer, "my husband don't believe in going abroad. 'We fetched her here, to this beautiful country spot, what could be better than that?' my husband says, and I can't budge him." A nice lady she were, but no gumption to her. So the end of it were that little Grace died —buried in the graveyard here, she be, under the red may tree—and *then* the family shifted off to Somerset, Tiverton way, for 'twas too sad for them here, the memory of her; they'd all been mortal fond of young Grace.

Tell them about little Nym, no, I didn't; anyway, if I had, they'd never have beleft me.

After the Kellaways left, six month went by, but, come May, when the bluebells and pheasant-eyes are out in the orchard, along comes a new lot. Yanks, these ones are; Spooner, the name is, and the chap, Professor Spooner, has hisself a job teaching social science over the Down at Portsbourne University. Then there's his lady and their daughter, little Brooke. That's a funny name to give a girl, I reckon, but Mrs Spooner telled me 'tis an old family name. Different to all the rest, they don't have a big tribe of kids, only the one little maid. "We'd ha' liked more," Mrs Spooner telled me, "but it wasn't to be." Friendly, talkative lady, Mrs Spooner, and powerful keen on old churches; she'd be out and about, all over the county, looking inside of 'em and taking brass rubbings. No, she don't take little Brooke along with her. "Brooke has her hobbies as I have mine," she says. "American children learn to be independent of their parents early on, Mr Standen." Independent is one thing, thinks I, left alone for hours on end is another; to be sure there was a Danish gal in the house, did the cooking, Uttë they called her. Deuce a bit of time did she ever spare from her housework and her fancy health magazines to look after the kid. "Is not my job," says she, when I carries in a basket of broccoli. "They hire me as cook, not as nurse." So young Brooke runs wild in the garden and woods, and I worry about her, special when I begin to notice she looks pale, and not as lively as she done when they first come to the place. Coughs a bit, now-and-now.

Ought I tell Miz Spooner about little Nym, tell her the place is death for a kid (and they with only the one) tell her to get the pize outa there afore 'tis too late and they're sorrier than sorry? Days I spend all of a bivver, wondering what's best to do.

Blishen and Pankhurst won't thank me for giving the house a bad name. Like as not, I'll be given my leaf to go. And who's to keep any sort of an eye on young Brooke *then*?

Skinny little 'un she were, not floppy like poor Grace but wiry and windshook; she liked to climb trees, and soon skinned her knees on most o' the big ones in the garden.

First, little Nym didn't trouble her. *I* could feel him, though, a-standing off, watching; in rain or sun, fog or shine, he'd be there; studying and wondering. But then he begun to move in, trying to make her notice him. That were the time I dreaded; when the air round the place begin to buzz, like it do before a storm, when the glass creeps down and down, you can feel a heaviness, there's midges a-biting and the birds fly low.

What I said, little Nym didn't mean no *harm*, but he had to make his mark someway, poor young devil, he was main set to make folk mind him. And his own kin, his older brothers and sisters, all so plim and personable, they'd never neighbour-together with him.

Stony-hearted lot, they musta been. To have treated him the way they done, in the end.

"I'm puzzled by Brooke's cough," Miz Spooner she says to me. "Where can she have picked it up? There's no kids in the village—more's the pity—Dr Venables assures me the air here is very healthy—she's never had such a brontical cough before. I can't understand it."

Dry, short cough it was; shook her poor little thin chest.

"We're going to try letting her sleep in the Garden Room," says Miz Spooner. "Dr Venables thinks that a good plan; that way she'll get plenty of fresh air."

I didn't think that were such a grand notion, but nobody asked my advice. The Garden Room had been built on by the Mildenhalls—or the Blakeneys—on the side o' the house facing the shrubberies and Harry Neale's hundred-acre field. It was mostly glass, glass walls and glass shutters that would open.

They set up a cot-bed in there for young Brooke. She liked it fine.

"I can hear the birds so loud and the hedgehogs grunting. It's great to have my own door."

There's a glass door, leads straight out on to the lawn. "I can get out real early," says Brooke.

She could get out real late, too. One evening I'd come back after me dinner to do a bit of watering. Bone-dry that May weather were, not a drip of rain fell the livelong month. I'd come back to give my young pea-plants a drenching. Owl-light, it were, with a bit of a glim in the sky. You could just see across the grass.

Professor and Mrs Spooner were away over the Down at

one of his college meetings, and the Danish girl indoors somewhere with her eyes pinned to the telly.

I knew I'd have the garden to myself—apart from little Nym, that is. I gets on with my watering and prensly the moon comes up. Print moonlight, 'twere. Then I was fair dumbfoundered to see the Garden Room door open, and young Brooke come a-wandering out dressed in her night-things.

"Now then, Missy," I start in to say, " 'tis time young'uns like you oughta be abed and asleep—" and then, dannel me, I sees that asleep she *be*, though her eyes be open; she don't heed me no more than if I was a rose-bush, but goes mouching along, over the lawn to the cedar tree; I follows her, all in a twit, case she start in to climb the tree, for, thinks I, I'll be obleeged to wake her then, 'tis too dangerous; but I'd allus heard it's best *not* to wake folk that go a sleep-walking, if you can someway coax and gentle 'em back to bed.

"Back to by-land, now, sweetheart," I says, no louder than a huss of wind, and young Brooke she mutters, "Wait—wait—" kind of busyfied and sidy, as if she were on an urgent errand and couldn't be fussed with me just then.

The cedar has big twin trunks and a crack betwixt 'em; young Brooke stuck her skinny arm into this crack, clear up to the shoulder, as if she were a-seeking for a thing she'd laid there and knew just where 'twas; sure enough, she pulled out her fist with summat in it—'bout the size of a crab-apple, 'twere; and then, calm as a clock, she turned her round and backwent softly over the grass and into the Garden Room again. I followed along, mortial curious to see what she'd took out of the tree, and found she'd laid her down on the bed again, still fast asleep, still clutching the thing in her bony little fist. Covered in bark-muck, 'twas, and mildew, but I could see it were an old broken mug, lustrous pink in colour, with speckles of gold.

My heart did thunder at that, I can tell ye. For well I recollects the story of little Nym.

Quiet as I'd tweak up a groundsel, I slipped it out of her hand, but at that she stirred and cried out, "No! No!" right anxious.

"Don't you fret, sweetheart, 'tis here on the chair," I says, and that calms her down; she goes to sucking her thumb like a two-year-old. So I covers her up and tiptoes away, locking the door behind me, goes round to the kitchen and hands the key to the Danish gal, who's in her own little parlour studying *Glamour* magazine.

"The young'un's been a sleepwalking," I says to her. "Best ye keep an eye on her and be sure to tell the missus."

Uttë just shrugs, as if 'tis no matter to her, takes the key, and goes back to her book.

Next day I comes up purposely to see Miz Spooner, but the gal tells me she and the gentleman are off to London for an educational conference and won't be back till termorrer. That did put me in a frit.

"Leaving none to care for the liddle maid?" says I.

"She gets her meals reg'lar," says the gal, a bit huffy. "I don't see as you've any call to set yourself in a hoe about her."

I could see I'd get no good out of that one, so I goes looking for young Brooke and found her by my potting shed where there's a water-butt. She'd got the water running from the spile and was rinsing the broken pink mug she'd fetched outa the cedar, doing it as careful and thorough as if 'twas a piece of Crown Derby she'd come by.

"What's that you have there, my love?" says I. And when she answers, my heart fair come into my mouth.

"It ain't mine," she says. "It b'longs to that boy I see standing outside my glass door at night-time. I'm a-rinsing it for him."

"Boy, what boy?"

Not that I doesn't know full well.

But he never *showed* hisself before.

"He stands at my door and looks in. I seen him a plenty times," says Brooke.

"We better hang a curtain over that door, then, my deary. It ain't right he should look in your private room."

"Oh, he could see through a curtain, I bleeve," says she. "What's his name, Mr Standen?"

"His name, deary?" I was all of a vlother, didn't know whether to answer or not. "Why, his name's little Nym," I told her in the end. For I reckon she was bound to find out.

That day was the first of June and, like it often happen, the weather turned over. From being bone dry, it went to dank and dripply, misty and moist—the kind of weather little Nym liked best. Maybe his elders, his brothers and sisters that was so hard on him, maybe they didn't fare out o'doors when it was wet; maybe then he had the garden to hisself.

And young Brooke was the same. Try as I would, I couldn't get her to stay indoors, with her storybooks and games, where she'd be safe from him.

"Where we come from in America, it's on the edge of the desert, ye see, the Mohave Desert, Mr Standen. We don't get foggy weather like this. I think it's beautiful. You can see things that look like ghosts, and the trees are mysterious."

She *would* stay out in the garden, all the day long, and sometimes I'd hear her coughing, and sometimes talking to herself.

Or was she talking to little Nym?

Come darkfall, when the Danish girl called her in to bed,

I bethought myself 'twould be best if I come up and slept there, in the garden. There's a middling small summerhouse, what Miz Spooner calls a Grotto, along at the far end of the grass plot, facing out to Tarbury Down. I made me up a bed with two-three old hop-sacks and laid me down there. 'Twasn't too handy, for it faced away from the garden, so I couldn't see what befell there, besides it being a black clungy night. But I slept light enough, waking every half-hour or so; then I'd doddle out to look in at the Garden Room glass door, and make sure was the liddle 'un sleeping as she ought. And the first five or six times I looked in, there she lay, quiet as a pitcher of flint.

Then—I dunno how come, I reckon I musta been fair rasped out with worriting—I buzzled off into a deep slumber. And what woke me next was lights and voices all across the garden, and folk rowsting about every which way, and a lot o' turmoil and tarrification.

Forth I went—'twas still dark as the inside of a cow—and found Professor Spooner and his lady and two-three other folks, all a-hunting and a-searching, with lanterns and torches, all of 'em calling high and low: "Brooke! Brooke! Where are you? My honey, where are you? Come to us, darling—come to us, Brooke!"

Then Miz Spooner catches sight 'o me. "Oh, Mr Standen, is that you?" she says, all of a pather. "Brooke's not in her bed and we're so dreadfully worried about her. Sir Barnholt told us such things—oh, Mr Standen, have you seen her?"

"No, Marm, I haven't," says I truly enough. "Last time I peeked in the Garden Room—about an hour since—she were sleeping fair enough."

I noticed Professor Spooner give me an old-fashioned look. "And what are *you* a doing here, Standen, so late at night?" he starts in to say. But then I see one of the gentlemen with him is Sir Barnholt Weller, as was dad of little Tom what broke his neck. A dentical downright chap, Sir Barney were, with a good headpiece, and a good friend to me, spite of all his trouble.

"Why, it's Sam Standen," he says, kind as can be. "We're main worried about young Brooke, Mr Standen. Can you help us?"

Seems Sir Barnholt met the Spooners in London, at this-here conference, they got to talking about the house, and what he told them put them in such a frit that they come bustling home directly, 'stead of biding in London overnight as they planned.

"Oh, Mr Standen, where can she *be*?" says Mrs Spooner, with the tears a flowing down. "Where do you think she can have gone?"

"Likely not far, Marm, but 'tis best we hunt quickly," says I, minding me of the lily pool. So we rake that through, all of a quake, but, thanks be, she ain't there, nor up any of the trees nor among the shrubs. Then I bethinks me of the compost heap—which, if I hadn't had my wits dazzled by being woke so sudden, I'd have thought of first. A main big, hot, yeasty heap it be, piled up against the brick wall by the glasshouses. Lawn-grass sweypings, leaves, weeds, and kitchen garbage, all stacked up and up like a layer cake. Wonderful fine compost that do furnish, after two-three years; black as Christmas pudden, it go.

Like I say, I run to the compost heap and, right away, I can see it's been paunched about and bruk up.

"You don't think she can be under *there*—surely, Mr Standen?" gulps the lady, who's close behind me.

I scoop it up, careful, with my hands; and there, sure enough, she be; buried an arm's-length under, all in among the grass brishings and mixen, and orange peel, and cabbage leaves.

"*Oh God!* She's not dead—is she?" says Mr Spooner, coming up.

The pile's so sweltering hot, on account o' the fermentation, that the young 'un feels warm as an oven bun and 'tis hard to tell for a minute, but Sir Barnholt feels for her pulse and finds it still going, but terrible slow; half stifled she'd been, under all that gouch. Didn't we got there when we had, she'd not have lived another half hour, says the doctor who had charge of her after the ambulance took her off to hospital. Oxygen, she were given, and needle shots for shock, and her mum and dad half mazed with worry, declaring they'd not spend another week in the house.

For the police had come, and studied the compost heap, and proved that no one except the young one herself had touched it. She'd climbed in and covered herself up, all by her lone, pulling the brishings down on top of her. In her sleep, it was thought. How could they stay in the house where such a thing might happen again?

But young Brooke confounds 'em.

When she comes home, two days after, and hears how they plan to flit, as soon's they can find another place, she fair bursts out crying.

I was there, as it come about.

She was lying out on a sofy under the big cedar and her ma sitting by her as if she'd never take her eyes off again. I happened by with my barrer full of weeds and hear her cry out.

"Move from here? Move *away*? But Ma, little Nym! Poor, poor little Nym! He's my friend! I promised him I'd not leave him!"

"My darling child, how can we stay here? This house is too dangerous for children.—And who, tell me, is little Nym?"

Brooke turns to me and says, "Mr Standen can tell you about little Nym, I bleeve."

So I telled the lady. How little Nym was the runt and weakling of the family, how his elders hated him, on account of he'd been his ma's death. And acos he were ugly and titchy. So they treated him hard and cruel, never played with him or spoke to him; hit and cuffed him and shut him up in cupboards; some days he'd get naught to eat all day. And the famous father had no notion of what were going on; no more notion than if he'd lived in the moon. Never spoke a word to his young 'uns from one week's end to another, by all accounts.

So, one time, accidental-ways, little Nym bust his sister Louisa's pink mug that she set great store by. And they was bound to punish him for that. As it chanced the bishop of Southease was coming to stay at the house, which were a great honour, for their Pa had newly been made a Lord. The other ones were set that young Nym mustn't get to see the bishop, nor his reverince discover they'd such an ugly, puny marred little brother; accordingly, to hide him away, they buried him in the muck-heap and told him he weren't on any account to come out until after the bishop had come and gone. Threatened to wring his neck if he done so.

And the end of it was, at the end of the day, somebody looked for little Nym and found him stifled and dead, under all the muck.

Tarrible scandalised folk were, to find out what had been going on in that fine big house, with so many servants, and the famous father shut away in his study.

"Poor, *poor* little boy," says Miz Spooner, a-wiping her eyes. "But, my honey, you do see why we can't *possibly* stay on here—why, you'd be walking in your sleep again, and little

Nym would think up some other dreadful thing to happen to you."

"No, no, Ma," says young Brooke, patient and calm. "Little Nym's my *friend* now. Don't you see? We was there, in the grass heap, so cosy together. And he telled me all that happened to him. And I said how sorry I was for him. And I promised I'd be his friend. See: there he is now."

While she talked, she'd been a setting out a dolls' tea-service she'd made, from acorn cups and walnut shells and lily pads, on the little table by her sofy. Now she pushes the broken pink mug on a lily pad to the other side of the table, and, says she, "Won't you take a cup of tea, little Nym?"

The Traitor

Oh yes—I once lived in a house with a ghost (said the old lady, gazing steadfastly into the red fire)—in fact with several ghosts. And they took no notice of me. It taught me a most painful lesson, one that I am not likely to forget.

It happened in the year when a great many small local libraries closed through lack of funds, and a lot of librarians were suddenly looking for jobs. I was one of them. Middle-aged lady librarians were two-a-penny, and nobody seemed particularly anxious for my services. I have always been rather solitary, from childhood on, without friends or relations—I will explain why in a minute; and in this difficulty I hardly knew where to turn. But fortunately, just at that point, I saw the advertisement in *The Lady*: 'Elderly gentlewoman seeks pleasant companion with a predilection for reading aloud.'

Now reading aloud has always been one of my greatest pleasures; first, with my dear mother when we had very few other resources; and then in Birklethwaite Library, where I ran a regular Reading Circle in the children's section twice a week, for I don't know how many years, and enjoyed it fully as much as any of my listeners.

So I wrote to the Box Number of the elderly gentlewoman, was interviewed, and happily we both took a liking to one another. She was, indeed, a most delightful person, wholly alert, although in her eighties, intelligent and humorous, in appearance a mixture of owl and eagle, with piercing dark eyes, a small beaky nose and wayward hair standing up on end like white plumes. What she thought of me, I do not know, except that it was sufficiently well to offer me the post, above a number of other applicants; what I thought of *her* was that I should immensely enjoy her company, and probably learn a great deal from her too. It was arranged that I should commence my duties in two months' time.

Mrs Crankshaw's surroundings were as pleasing as her personality: she lived in a Georgian mansion called Gramercy Place under the slopes of the South Downs, and I looked forward to unlimited walks in the surrounding countryside during my free hours; but to my disappointment, before it was time to take up residence with my new employer, I had a letter informing me of a change of plan.

The poor lady had suffered a slight stroke. 'Nothing of consequence, I am already better, apart from being confined, at present, to a wheelchair,' she wrote with characteristic firmness, 'but I have decided that it would be practical to move to a less solitary environment—better for you, too, my dear Miss Grey. My lawyers are hard at work on the purchase of another house in a small agreeable town—in fact, the purchase of *three* houses which will be converted into one, so that, if we have less outdoors, we shall have plenty of *in*doors, and shall not be on top of one another, which I think is most important. The builders are only waiting for completion to start tearing down partitions, and I trust that our original plans will be put back by no more than a month or two.'

She did not mention the name of the small agreeable town, and I waited with interest to learn where it was, confident that our tastes would coincide in this, as they had in other matters.

The purchase went through, but the building work dragged, as such work always does, and it was more like nine weeks before Mrs Crankshaw was able to transfer herself from the nursing home, and her furniture from Gramercy Place, and write to me that she was ready for me to come and take up my duties in the new residence.

When she did so, the address gave me a shock—the first of several. For she wrote from The Welcome Stranger, Stillingley; and Stillingley was the town where I had spent my childhood, after my father had gone to prison.

And when I reached my destination I received the second shock. For The Welcome Stranger turned out to be the house where my mother and I had lived, now joined together with the houses on either side of it.

"They were all for sale, so I bought the whole little old Tudor row," said Mrs Crankshaw comfortably. "Luckily my brother's legacy gave me plenty of leeway. (I told you, didn't I, that he had died, and left me some money?) And it is right that the houses should be joined together again, for, apparently, back in the seventeenth century, the whole building was one large inn; only in those days it was called The Bull. But since there is already a Bull Inn in the town, I thought I would choose another old coaching-house name. Besides, it is prettier. The coach entrance was that archway that runs through to the yard at the back."

I could have told her that. I could have told her a great deal more. I had spent thirteen years in that street, in the middle house, and knew every crooked step in it, every beam and cranny, as well as the palm of my own hand. It was wonderful how little the builders had changed; as Mrs Crankshaw said, the building had been one house two hundred years before; all they needed to do was to knock down a few partitions.

The third and worst shock came as we were having our first cup of tea in the white-panelled parlour—which had been my mother's study where, three days a week, she worked at translation, and read proofs for publishers (on the other three days she had an editorial job on the local paper).

I had asked Mrs Crankshaw why she picked this particular town, did she have any connections with it?

"Oh yes," she said, tranquilly sipping her Lapsang Souchong. "My brother lived here, in Pallant House, for a number of years. I used to visit him, and always thought it would be a pleasant place in which to settle if, for some unfortunate reason, one was debarred from living out in the real country. My brother was a judge, you may have heard of him: Sir Charles Sydney."

And of course I had heard of him. He was the judge who had sentenced my father. That was why my mother had moved to the town, after father had gone to prison. Firstly we had to give up our own house, we could not afford it. Secondly, visiting would be easier – only an hour's bus-ride to the jail where Father was serving his twenty-five-year sentence. But also, having learned, during the trial, that Stillingley was where Sir Charles lived, my mother, apparently at that time, nursed some obscure notion of meeting him in the street or in the Pallant Gardens, or after church on Sunday, and trying to make an appeal to him. "For anyone can see that he is a *good* man," she repeated over and over, with tears in her eyes, "and your father is a good man too; nobody denies that. Somehow, somehow, there *must* be some way of getting his sentence annulled, or at least reduced—I am sure there must be."

But this plan came to nothing, because, firstly she never ran into Sir Charles or plucked up the courage to approach him. I think he was a very busy man, hardly ever to be seen in the streets of the town, mostly up in London. And, secondly, after serving only two years of the sentence, my father died; of a broken heart, Mother said. I sometimes think it is just as well that he did not live on into the times of glasnost and perestroika and the end of the Cold War; all that has happened since his conviction makes what he did—sending some not very important scientific information to a colleague in Moscow—seem so pitifully trifling. My father was a Civil Servant, and of course what he did was strictly forbidden, and counted as treason. But he was a man of tremendously high principles, a pacifist and a Conscientious Objector; and he felt strongly that all scientific information should be shared equally all over the world. So he was prepared to go to prison for his beliefs. He took himself and his principles to prison; and he left me and Mother out in the cold. Or rather, he left me in prison too . . .

I often thought that he had behaved very unfairly to Mother and me. Either he should not have married and had a family, or he should have chosen some other job. I was only five when he was taken off, and I missed him dreadfully for a number of years. He had been a kind, affectionate father, and used to play lots of games with me. One was called Treasure Islands, a guessing game, trying to find out about each other's treasures; and we told long sagas, each taking up the story in turn; or we did cookery, inventing new dishes from a list of ingredients all beginning with the same letter: apples, anchovies, artichokes, arrowroot . . . Heartburn Holidays, father used to call those afternoons.

So it was an incurable grief when he vanished away to prison, and a worse one when he died. Mother never married again. She and I reverted to her maiden name of Grey when we moved to Stillingley, because she used to get a lot of hate letters from people who said that Father was a traitor. People seem to have unlimited time for acts of spite to other people who have never done them any personal harm. And about ten years after Father's death, Mother also died. And I took a course in librarianship with the small amount of money she left me, and became a librarian, and worked in libraries for twenty-five years. After Mother's death I never went back to Stillingley. We had no close friends there, because of the quiet life she chose to lead, so it was not at all probable that anybody in the town would recognise me. (Nobody did; partly because the town had changed a great deal. All the little old corner shops had gone, and instead there were tourist boutiques. Walking about the familiar streets. I felt like a ghost myself.)

So, my dears, I expect you can understand why, when Mrs Crankshaw said, "My brother was a judge: Sir Charles Sydney," I did not at once and honestly exclaim: "Why, he was the judge who sentenced my father to twenty-five years for sending treasonable communications to Soviet Russia," but instead gulped, bit my tongue, knelt to lay another log on the fire, and kept quiet.

Oh, what a difference it would have made if I had not done so! If I had told her that this house was my childhood home. For, once having embarked on a policy of concealment, I was, of course, obliged to go on; there never came an opportunity to change my mind, toss discretion aside, and proclaim: "Oh, by the way, Mrs Crankshaw, I forgot to mention, when we moved in, that your brother sent my father to prison." That seemed out of the question. And, although I had never in any way blamed her brother—who was only doing his duty, acting on his principles, as Father had acted on his—there was no slightest hint of resentment or anything of that kind —yet, nevertheless, the fact that I was keeping this major secret from her had some kind of crimping or smothering effect on our relationship; happy and friendly although that became.

Well—it *must* have, mustn't it?

But the worst result of all was what I am now going to tell you.

When Mother and I first arrived to live at Middle House, we were busy carrying baskets and jugs and suitcases in through the back door, when I was a little dismayed to observe an eye carefully scanning us from the window of the house next door. And when I say an eye, I mean literally nothing *but* an eye: the bottom left-hand corner of the lace curtain was twitched aside, leaving just room for one muddy grey optic to peer sharply over the window-sash and study our possessions.

This gave a decidedly chilly, sinister impression; it could not have been more misleading.

After a day or two spent in getting settled, we began to receive the impression that there was a tremendous amount of back-and-forth, come-and-go, to-and-fro, between the two little houses on either side of us. Upper House, Middle House, and Lower House, the row was called. We occupied Middle House; Upper and Lower Houses appeared to be inhabited by two couples who could not have enough of each other's company. Mr and Mrs Brown, Mr and Mrs Taylor were their names, we learned from the postman; and we soon discovered why they all lived in one another's pockets—it was because Mrs Taylor and Mrs Brown were sisters. In no time at all they had invited us into their highly polished front rooms, resplendent with pot plants and cage birds, and they had given us their life histories. Mrs Taylor and Mrs Brown—Di and Ruby—were cockneys, had originally been evacuated to Stillingley in World War One, had fallen in love with local boys, married them, and never returned to London. Their husbands, Fred Taylor and Jim Brown, were, respectively, a bus driver and a builder's foreman. By the end of three weeks, they were playing a very important part in our lives. Fred, every two days, used to bring us fish from Portsbourne, which was at the end of his bus run, and was a monument of sense and experience when it came to practical matters. Jim could deal with any household emergency, could fix leaking taps or loose wiring, mend windows, replace fallen tiles. Ruby and Di supplied the light relief; especially Di. She was a stand-up comic, a harlequin of a woman. Not at all good-looking, she was lean and rangy, with vigorously permed pale-grey locks and skin like uncooked frozen pastry. It was her eye that had peered from under the curtain in Ruby's kitchen. The sisters were perpetually in and out of each other's houses, exchanging pots or clothes, borrowing salt or soap, telling jokes or gossip. "Roo? Are you there, Roo? Got a minute? Come and take a look at this! Di! Di! Got a pinch of bicarb—a few mothballs—a forty-watt bulb—a spoonful of honey?"

Although the husbands had relatives in the town—plenty of them—the two couples formed such a compact group in themselves that they hardly required other company. But they were immensely, infinitely kind to Mother and me. They became our family—surrogate uncles, aunts, grandparents, cousins. "You're so *different* from us!" Di sometimes said wonderingly to Mother. That was because Mother spoke several languages and could translate from German and Russian. Our neighbours themselves had the unassuming modesty, the simple unobtrusive diffidence, of completely happy people. They saw no need to assert themselves; they already had all they required.

It was not long before Mother had told them everything about Father's prison sentence. She had resolved never to mention this circumstance to a single soul in Stillingley; she disclosed it all to Ruby and Di, Jim and Fred, without the least hesitation. She did not even ask for their discretion; she knew by instinct that they would never mention the matter to anybody; and they never did.

They listened to her tale with wondering sympathy, wholly without passing judgement.

"Well: he had to do what he thought right, didn't he?" said Fred.

"And so did the judge; all the same, it does seem a proper shame," said Jim.

"All that time away from you; it's like as if you were a widder," sighed Ruby.

"And poor little Snowball here, so many years without her dad," grieved Di.

From then on they were even kinder to us.

Trip-trap and clitter-clatter through my childhood run the feet of Ruby and Di back and forth outside our dining-room window. "Di! Ruby! Listen to this! Can you let me have a lump of dripping? Come and look at the bird, Di! D'you think he's poorly?"

They insisted on our sharing in the products of all their activities, marmalade, chutney, pickled onions.

Soon it was: "Missis Grey? Are you busy? Can you spare a minute?" And quickly the Mrs Grey gave way to "Ianthe" (which they shortened to "Ianth"). But, scrupulously, delicately, they never dropped in on my mother during the hours of daylight; Fred, the chieftain of the tribe, had decreed this. "She's the bread-winner, see? You gotta respect that and not go bothering her, you two, mind, while she's workin'."

Fred and Jim, Di and Ruby; they were like the biologist's ideal, a completely self-sufficient society without the need of any outside agency or supplies.

Only once a year, at Christmas, did they summon huge

hosts of other relatives whose arrival was heralded, weeks before, by monumental piles of Christmas cards which, as soon as they arrived, were slung on zigzag strings across and across the front rooms, in among the cyclamens, the tinsel, poinsettias, mistletoe, and folding paper bells. Then they had a Christmas party. After the first occasion, we carefully avoided those parties, which could last for six, seven, eight hours at a stretch; Mother explained that she really had to go on working over Christmas and could not afford all that time off.

"But what about the liddle 'un? *She* don't have to work."

"She's shy," said Mother firmly.

Those parties did indeed have a numbing, shattering effect, as one munched one's way through more and more sausage rolls and sandwiches, drank more and more lethal mixtures of alcohol and fruit juice, while trying to keep up a continuous fixed smile at the tireless crackle of repartee from cousins, nephews, uncles, and indestructible great-aunts. All these relatives adored and respected our quartet, and would have liked to be invited much more often than once a year. "But we don't want 'em," said Fred, Ruby, Di, or Jim. "We're comfortable just on our loney-own, thank you *very* much—with Ianth and the young 'un."

So time passed for us, peacefully enough; we were buttressed, comforted, and contained by the strong dependable structure on either side.

When I was seven my father died in jail and, during that time, Fred was of silent, sterling support to my mother. He rented a car and drove her to and fro during Father's illness; he drove her to the crematorium, sternly excluding his wife, brother-in-law, and sister-in-law. "No, she don't want you lot; it's a family occasion, see?" And he himself would have stayed outside the chapel if she had not insisted on his coming in, and then he stayed firmly on his own at the back. A surprising number of other people turned up, Mother told me (I was in bed at the time with measles); there were quite a few journalists, and old friends from past days. Mother was glad to dodge them after the ceremony and take refuge with Fred in the rented Rover.

That night my mother and the four neighbours held a kind of wake for Father. I expect she felt she owed it to them; it was what they would have expected. Fruit cake, cold ham, sherry, and whisky; lying upstairs in bed, feverish, with painfully aching ears and throat, I heard the subdued hum and grumble of voices down below gradually grow more cheerful, an occasional laugh ring out.

"How can they?" I thought, thrashing and tossing in bed, wretched, sick and furious. Fred came up with a jug of lemonade and found me so, tears hissing on my hot red cheeks like water on the surface of an iron.

I glared at him, kept by manners and convention from saying what I felt.

But he understood perfectly well.

"I know, I know," he said, settling his stocky bulk down with caution on my cane-seated chair. "You think we're all heartless down there, don't you, tellin' jokes to your mum and makin' her laugh? But she's done a deal of sorrowin' already, and she's got a deal more to do; she needs a bit of a break. It ain't unfair to your dad; I expect he'd do the same. I daresay he liked a bit of a laugh in his time, didn't he? I expect he told you a good few jokes?"

Reluctantly I nodded.

"Well then," said Fred. "Just you remember, dearie; death ain't all black plumes and caterwauling. You got to carry on as best you can."

*

Fred saw us through various other troubles. When our cat died, he helped bury her; when my first boyfriend dropped me, left me a stricken thirteen-year-old grass-widow, he managed to make me believe there were as good fish in the sea, which helped at the time, though in fact he was wrong, for I never acquired another.

And then, when I was fifteen, Di died. She had been growing gradually thinner and more gaunt; there was less vivacity in her jokes. She underwent an operation; spent painful weeks in bed at home, tended by Mother and Ruby. Then Fred said to me one day: "I've got to tell you this fast—we're going to lose her," and bolted blindly out of our kitchen. He himself was losing weight at a rapid rate; after her death he became, suddenly, a shrunken thread of a man. Ruby and Jim took him into their house, as they said he shouldn't be on his own. By this time I was sixteen, about to go off on a residential course at the other end of England. Fred was in bed, ill, when I left; I kissed him goodbye and never saw him again. Jim soon followed; it was as if, once the structure and symmetry of the group had been damaged, its individual members were vulnerable, badly at risk. Jim died of bronchitis, coughing his lungs away. He had been a heavy smoker. Poor Ruby could not bear her life without the others around her.

"It just don't seem right," she said to Mother. She developed a heart trouble and died in the ambulance on the way to hospital. Now the houses on either side of us were up for sale; and one day, at my residential college, I received a telegram to say that my mother had died of pneumonia, very suddenly, in the local hospital. Like Ruby, she was unable to manage without the rest of the group to support her.

After letting Middle House for a couple of years, to support me through my training, I sold it, having no wish to return there. New neighbours were installed on either side. The thought of Upper House without Fred and Di, of Lower House without Jim and Ruby, of our own house without my mother, was not to be borne, I would have felt like a survivor from a holocaust. I found a plain job elsewhere, in a plain library in a plain provincial town, and entrenched myself in books, catalogues, indexes, and reading aloud.

Until the day, over twenty years later, when I found myself back there, installed in The Welcome Stranger, with Mrs Crankshaw.

She, in her wheelchair, professed herself wholly delighted with the three houses fashioned into one. The builders had made ramps for her, so that her domain was entirely on the ground floor, bedroom at one end, living space in the middle, kitchen at the other. So her living quarters were constructed from Mother's and my old kitchen dining-room, where Ruby and Di had clattered continually past the window. Her bedroom was Ruby's front room, where the terrifying Christmas parties had taken place. I could sit reading *Dr Thorne* aloud to Mrs Crankshaw and think of all those spangled cards fluttering overhead, and Fred's nephew Peter rolling his eyes under the mistletoe. My bedroom was upstairs (my own old bedroom, as it fell out) and there I lay at night, listening to the house creak and rustle gently round me; Mrs Crankshaw had installed gas-fired central heating.

After a few weeks, Mrs Crankshaw said to me, "Miss Grey—Lucy—I am quite delighted with this house, and with our arrangement; I hope that you are too? But would you say—entirely without prejudice—that the place is slightly haunted?"

"No one has said anything of the kind to me, Mrs Crankshaw," I fenced.

"Oh, won't you call me Moira, my dear, don't you think we have reached that stage by now? No, of course I had no such intimation from the agents or the lawyers or the builders —but then, one never does, does one? Just the same, I do begin to wonder. During the last twenty years there seem to have been a great many occupants. Do you think it was because no one cared to stay very long?"

It was true that, since the time of Jim and Ruby, Fred and Di and my mother, the three little houses had changed hands repeatedly. Nobody seemed to have stayed more than a year or so.

"But that need not mean a thing," I argued, quite truly. "The whole town is in a—a state of transition. House prices are rising so fast, people buy them as investments, do them up, and move on. Also, the place is becoming more of a tourist centre than it—than it probably was twenty years ago."

It was becoming harder and harder to maintain my pretence of never having lived in the town before. I felt worse and worse about it. Because our relationship—Moira's and mine—was, in all other respects, so happy, open, and free; she was beginning to seem like a beloved aunt, or cherished older sister; one of those relations I had never been blessed with. We were able to talk to one another about every possible topic—except one; and our reading-aloud sessions were periods of calm, undiluted pleasure.

"What is giving you the idea that the place might be haunted?" I asked with caution.

"Why, there are times—especially when you are reading to me, my dear—when I am almost convinced that I can hear *voices*—voices perhaps in the next room, or somewhere else about the house, or perhaps in the little lane at the back."

"Perhaps they are real voices?" I suggested hopefully. "Echoes, you know, from the lane."

The little lane—along which Ruby and Di used to run to

and fro all day—was a right-of-way and led to the public library, my long-ago haunt of comfort and instruction.

"Well, yes, sometimes they might be real," agreed Mrs Crankshaw, "but not always. Not late at night. And the voices inside the house *must* be ghosts—mustn't they? Unless I am going potty."

"And that you certainly are not, dear Mrs Crankshaw," I said fervently.

"Moira, my dear—Moira." Her hawk-eyes gleamed.

"What *kind* of voices do you think you hear?"

"You are sure you don't hear them yourself?" she inquired wistfully.

"No, I'm afraid I don't. Not at present. Perhaps I shall, by and by."

Oh, how I wished this! For she said, "Well, there are several different voices. That's why I'm sure it can't be just my imagination—for I never was very imaginative, you know, even as a child, I was the most prosaic little creature, and never cared particularly for pretend games or fairy stories. How could I invent something like this? What I hear is most often women's voices—quite raucous and cheerful, with a cockney twang to them. Not a bit like our good neighbours up and down the hill."

The good neighbours up and down the hill were nearly all antique dealers, who went in for a good deal of packaged refinement and ersatz chumminess; the females wore tweeds, and the males neatly-trimmed beards.

"And you hear the voices particularly when I am reading to you?"

"Yes, is that not curious? It is precisely like—you know when you tune into a radio station, and at first it comes through perfectly clear, and then, by degrees, some foreign station comes in and jams it; though that is not quite the case here, for I can always hear you, my dear Lucy, perfectly well—but then in the background the voices begin."

"Always women's?"

"No; the women are the most frequent, but occasionally I get male voices farther back—two different ones, I am fairly sure, one quite deep-toned and gruff, the other higher and more nasal."

"Can you hear what they *say*?" I asked with quivering interest.

"Not yet, my dear. But let us hope that in due course I shall! Really, nothing so interesting has happened to me for years—and I am sure that I owe it all to your company in this pleasant place, my dear Lucy; I am so very happy that we had the luck to find each other."

Her words filled me with mingled guilt and relief. Relief that she appeared to be deriving so much pleasure and interest from the phenomenon; many old ladies might have felt very differently; guilt that it was too late for me to be more candid and forthcoming about my friends; I felt I was doing them serious injustice by not telling her all about them.

Oh, what a tangled web we weave! . . .

While Mrs Crankshaw kept exclaiming in her satisfaction at what a warm, welcoming atmosphere the place had—"Just like its name! I christened better than I knew!" I, perhaps because I found myself in such a curious moral dilemma, felt the house curiously cold and unresponsive. No echoes came back to me, not a sound, not a signal, from the happy childhood hours I had passed there. And some of them *had* been happy: moments of hope, before my father died, moments of peace and companionship when my mother and I read aloud *Villette* or *War and Peace* in late spring evenings with a pale moon looking solemnly in at my bedroom window; moments of triumph when I had done well at school; or moments of pure fun when Di and Ruby were clowning and Fred and Jim, with us, were laughing at them.

I could not escape the impression that the house was displeased with me. I should have come clean; and I had not.

Mrs Crankshaw began to have remarkable dreams.

"I see such faces! Such real characters! Can they be people whom I have met, at some point during my life, and completely forgotten? They seem so extremely real. There is one extraordinary woman—a tall, bony, angular creature, with false teeth, and such a laugh! I have dreamed about her several times. Her name is Vi or Di—something like that. I must say, she is very entertaining. I wonder if I can be developing mediumistic powers in my old age? I must talk to the Vicar about it."

She talked to the Vicar, but he was new and young; had come to the town long since the days of Fred and Jim and Ruby and Di. He could make nothing of Mrs Crankshaw's dreams. He assured us that, so far as he knew, nobody had experienced anything of this kind in the house.

I thought, also, that Mrs Crankshaw might be developing mediumistic powers. Was what was happening a kind of telegraphic flash passing over from my memory to hers? Was she picking up scenes from my past—my carefully suppressed past—and, as it were, printing them off in the darkroom of her mind? Did she see these things because I was there?

Or was she receiving entirely new impressions? Were the ghosts of Jim and Fred, of Di and Ruby, still floating around, still present in the house—disturbed, perhaps, by my arrival, by the builders' work—available to Mrs Crankshaw because she was so happily, generously ready to receive them—but not choosing to reveal themselves to me?

That was indeed a chilling thought.

I could imagine—all too easily—Fred's quarter-deck

voice. (He had been a petty-officer once, long ago, before he retired from the navy and took to bus-driving.) I remembered how sternly he had said: "She's the bread-winner, see? You gotta respect that and not go bothering her, you two." I imagined him saying: "You shoulda told the lady the whole story, Snowball, right from the start. Now you put yourself in what they call a false position. And you put *us* in one too."

Oh how I longed to apologise, to confess, to have matters somehow set right!

One morning Mrs Crankshaw called to me, in a voice of pure astonishment:

"Lucy! Somebody pushed my wheelchair!"

Contrary to her hopes, she had never recovered the use of her legs; her upper body was active, but below her hips she was motionless. Because of the ramps, all the ground floor of the house was accessible to her; she had a self-propelled wheelchair with an inner and an outer wheel.

She could spin herself around, very easily, through her downstairs domain, and did so, all day long. It was only when we went out of doors that I pushed her. But the wheelchair had a self-activating brake, a locking device which automatically engaged when the chair came to rest, so that it could never accidentally roll.

"Somebody," said Mrs Crankshaw, with absolute conviction, "*some*body disengaged the brake and pushed me over to the front window."

"You are quite sure that you didn't, almost unconsciously, do it yourself?"

She thought about it. "No, my dear. Because my tiresome old fingers are growing so arthritic and stiff these days that, when I heard a horse's hoofs go clopping past outside, I did just wonder, would it be worth unlocking the brake and rolling myself over to take a look out of the window. But I decided not to bother—and then, you see, some kind agency did it for me!"

I felt—believe it or not—a prickle of jealousy.

I said, "Dear Mrs Crankshaw. I am so very sorry about your hands. Let me give them a rub with embrocation. And you know that, wherever I am about the house, if you give me a call, I'll always *gladly* come and move your chair—"

"Oh, my dear, I know you will! And my hands are nothing—a trifle. With so few disabilities, in this charming house and with your company, I am a very lucky old person. And now, it seems, I have a friendly ghost to push me about as well."

She laughed with real pleasure.

But I felt nervous. Bitterly ashamed, of course—for how could I possibly mistrust my kind friends enough to suppose that they might do Mrs Crankshaw any harm? Just the same, from then on, I kept a very sharp eye on the position of her chair, and would casually move stools or small tables into its possible path, so that it could never roll very far.

Several times, during the next few weeks, the chair was moved again, always to anticipate some vague wish that Mrs Crankshaw had hardly yet expressed, even to herself. "They positively forestall my needs," she said, laughing. "It really is *most* interesting, my dear Lucy. I am so *sorry* that you can't see them."

For now she was beginning to get a glimpse of them—in odd, short flashes.

"Rather like a flickering, faulty television screen," was how she expressed it. "And, yes, sometimes in colour, sometimes black-and-white. Colour comes most often at twilight—black-and-white during full daylight. At night they seem to fade completely—just the reverse of what one expects of ghosts."

Bit by bit, she described them.

"There is the tall, rangy woman. These are all quite modern spectres, my dear. No ruffs, or crinolines, or nonsense of that kind. The tall woman wears high-heeled leather kneeboots and a long narrow tube of a skirt, with an apron over it, and layers and layers of cardigans. Very often she has her hair in curlers. She is always the strongest image. Then there is a shorter woman, who nearly always has a piece of knitting in her hand."

Dear Ruby! The number of hideous fancy-stitch sweaters she had knitted me which I was obliged out of politeness (and need also) to wear until I had outgrown them.

"Then there is a stocky thickset man who wears a dark-blue uniform. Perhaps he is a postman? I get a feeling of great kindness and dignity. And a little gnome-like fellow who spends hours poring over a folded-up square inch of newspaper, and always has a cigarette dangling from his lip. He is the faintest of them—but still, he is growing clearer as the days go by."

"Just those four? No others?"

No grey-haired, thin-faced woman with horn-rimmed glasses, busy at her typewriter?

"No, you greedy creature," said Mrs Crankshaw, laughing. "Aren't four well-constructed honest-to-goodness spooks enough for you? *How* I wish my dear brother Charles were still alive; he used to be such a sceptical materialist, would never admit even the possibility of ghosts. What a good time I should have, telling him about mine! I really begin to feel as if they were my own family—my family of phantoms."

To hear her say that gave me a terrible twinge. And then she began to speak of writing to the *Psychic News*. "This is such an interesting phenomenon, my dear. I feel it should be shared with experts."

"But," I argued, "then they would want to come down and inspect and investigate, and put in watchers and try to take pictures with infra-red light—or however people do photograph ghosts; do you really want all that going on in your peaceful house?"

She glanced round the pleasant white-panelled parlour.

"Well, no," she conceded. "Perhaps not."

In fact, to me, the house was *not* peaceful any longer. It seemed to throb with reproof and reproach. I knew that the time had come when I must, I absolutely must confess all, and make a clean breast to Mrs Crankshaw.

And what a poor figure I was going to cut! Deceitful, dishonest, hypocritical, cowardly, dishonourable—but, above all, shabby and perfidious to my good friends. Was it so surprising that they seemed to have turned against me?

I decided to make my confession one evening, after our reading-aloud period, between tea and supper. That was our easiest, happiest time, when we were most completely in tune with one another; then, I thought, I would have the best chance of winning forgiveness and understanding from Mrs Crankshaw for my long course of deceit.

All day my heart rattled painfully inside my rib-cage. Mrs Crankshaw occupied herself as usual, in reading newspapers and political journals, in writing letters to her bed-bound friends, with sketching and solitaire and petit-point; she was a most self-sufficient person. Occasionally she would raise her eyes from the card-table or embroidery pillow to remark, "There goes the tall lady past the window, carrying a birdcage with a canary in it. Do canaries have ghosts too, poor little things?" Or, "Now I see the man in blue. He is carrying one of those rush baskets that fish used to be sold in; do you remember them? Do ghosts eat fish?"

Oh Fred, I thought. He would be bringing the fish for my

mother and me. Oh dear, *dear* Fred, why can't I see you too? I'll tell her this very evening. The minute that we have finished our stint on *Wuthering Heights*. And then perhaps, perhaps they will show themselves to me.

We had our reading session, installed as usual: Mrs Crankshaw on the sofa, comfortably snugged in, with cushions behind her and a rug over her knees; myself in the rocker with the table lamp at my side. Twilight was falling fast.

I read aloud several chapters. We were very close to the end.

"Shall I stop here?" I said nervously, clearing my throat.

"Oh no, *do* go on, my dear—if you are not becoming hoarse? Do finish the book. I don't know *how* many times I have read *Wuthering Heights*," said Mrs Crankshaw with satisfaction. "And it gets better every time."

"Are you—are you hearing the voices?" I asked.

"Just a little. They are chatting comfortably in the background. Not intrusively, you know—but like people in the next room who know that we shall stop our reading and talk to them by and by."

So I read on; read the last two chapters, came to the last line: "*I wondered how anyone could ever imagine unquiet slumbers for the sleepers in that quiet earth.*"

Closing the book, I let a silence of a few moments elapse. The room was almost dark now, apart from the bright circle of my reading light. I glanced about—hoping for a glimpse of a long tube skirt, a head of curlers, a pair of leather knee-boots, a dark-blue uniform jacket. But there was nothing.

"Mrs Crankshaw: there is something I have to tell you. Something I should have told you long ago, at the very beginning of our friendship. *Listen:*—"

But I had left it too late.

Mrs Crankshaw's head had fallen back peacefully on her cushion; her hands, relaxed, lay open on the rug. She had gone for good, and left me all alone in that silent, silent house.

Die from Day to Day

It seemed to him that he was a middle-aged man, tired and irritable, beset by many cares, both professional and domestic, driving his family back along the motorway. It seemed they had been spending a short and acrimonious holiday at a Joplins Super-Holiday Theme Park in Bridpool. Fun for the Kids, Relaxation for the Adults. Neither promise had been kept. The kids, three girls, had been bored, the adults had quarrelled. The hope had been that this holiday would repair their tottering marriage. The hope had withered on the stem.

"Can't you drive a bit faster, Ewart?" his wife cried impatiently. "We've had a rotten week, we might as well get home while the shops are open. And the girls still have their holiday homework to do."

His response was to drop his speed by five miles an hour. Eva pressed her lips together in fury, but kept silent. After a few minutes he said, sourly, "Why didn't they bring their homework with them?"

"Oh, Ewart! They did bring it, but there was never any time. Or any place to do it."

Casting his mind back, with reluctance, among the small circular glass tables scattered here and there in the purple-carpeted lounge areas, through the ever-howling storm of music, through the clattering crowded ranch-style eaterie, the comfie coffeeteria, the bunburger bakerie, and the solaroid sports salon, he was obliged to admit that what she said was no more than the truth. The children's bedroom had been simply a sleep area, with small basin and three-tiered bunk; the adult bedroom merely a space containing emperor-sized bed, obsessionally frilled, a tea-tray on legs, shower cabinet, and TV screen; the notion of work, reading or writing, was neither entertained at that place nor catered for.

"Holidays were different when I was a boy," he muttered, half to himself. "We did a lot of reading. We kept diaries."

"Oh, Dad! You and your Good Old Days. Always on about them."

"They *were* good," he asserted grumpily. "I'm telling you, if I were to be offered one day—just *one* day—from any one of those childhood holidays, I'd accept it even if it meant living through all the rest of my life, over again. And that's saying something!"

"It certainly is," his wife commented drily. "I wouldn't live through *my* life over again, not for the Golden Apples of the Whatdoyoucallem. Not for anything you could offer me."

Her voice was loaded with venom.

The girls in the back were, by now, as usual, scuffling over some toy. Voices were raised in dispute.

"Mine!"

"No, mine!"

"Ma, Lecky's gone and ruined it. She's broken it!"

"I like that. It was you who lost the washer!"

"Tish had the washer. She put it in her pocket."

"Well, I haven't got it now. You took it, Lecky."

"Oh, do be quiet, all of you!" shouted their father. "Or I'll stop the car and dump you all out on the hard shoulder."

"You couldn't *do* that!"

"You're not allowed!"

"It's illegal!"

"Quiet, girls, when your father tells you," said Eva, but without conviction, and she distributed biscuits, which produced a munching silence for a few minutes, followed by demands for drinks.

"We just passed the last service area," said Ewart. "There isn't another for forty miles."

He felt a sour satisfaction in being able to thwart them so completely.

"Should have filled the flask before we started. Or brought some juice."

The children returned to their wrangle about the washer, and he, to distract his thoughts from the disagreeable present, went back to the past.

Where had it been, that childhood paradise? North, east, or west? He had no idea. Memory had no clues to offer. There had been a stone-built cottage, slate-roofed; a sandy, pebbled turnaround for the car, a brook with a footbridge, a ford, through which the car had to splash. On some joyful occasions, when there had been heavy rain higher up the valley, they were marooned at the cottage until the water level went down. There was a rocky river, a gravel-bed, a pine-wood, a heather-covered hillside. There were trout in the river, owls at night, hares in the meadows. Mushrooms, found in dewy dawns. Hazelnuts, found in bird-haunted thickets.

There had been a companion who played with him, in the beechwoods, on the gravel-bed, building palaces, in the river, wading and jumping from rock to rock, swimming, retiring to the haybarn when it rained.

What had been her name?

She had been *the* companion, the perfect one, setting a standard, ideal, irrevocable, to which no one else could ever aspire; the prototype, the archetype, the paragon, the unattainable summit.

No other person, ever again, whether male or female, had supplied that perfection of fellowship.

What was her name? Who was she, where had she come from?

"Oh, do be quiet!" he cried to his quarrelling daughters. "Read your books, for heaven's sake, can't you? I've got a lot to worry about without your constant row."

"*Worrying* won't help," said Eva disagreeably.

"I like that!" he snapped at her. "You'll have to suffer too, you'll all suffer, if the case goes against me and I have to pay out thirty thousand to that woman. Money doesn't grow on trees."

"It doesn't grow on trees for *her*, either. Poor devil. After all, it was you who ran over her husband."

"He was drunk! Blotto! Falling about in the road like a bagatelle ball. It's just astonishing something of the kind hadn't happened to him months ago, years ago."

"It was just his bad luck that all the other drivers but you managed to avoid him," said Eva. The girls had stopped quarrelling to listen. "And now that poor woman is left to bring up her children on her own."

Was that a note of envy in her voice?

The motorway went snaking along, through empty country, between highish wooded hills, brownish-blue, bluish-brown, humped one behind the other, their outlines beginning to soften in the gathering dusk. There was very little other traffic at this time, at this season.

"And what about the other case?" said his wife. "When is that due to come to court?"

Now her voice definitely held a note of malicious amusement.

Ewart kept quiet, went on driving. One of the girls said:

"What other case, Ma?"

"Your father was so unfortunate as to wall a poor old lady up, alive, in her own house."

"He did what?"

"Oh, rubbish, Eva. What terrible rubbish you talk," he said angrily. "It was nothing like that, and you know it. You might at least not take pains to put the children against me, give them entirely erroneous ideas—"

"What happened, Ma? Tell us!"

"Damn it, Eva, I was only the council planning officer—you make it sound as if I, personally, boarded her up—"

"Ma, what happened?"

"If you ever looked at the papers you'd know about it," said Ewart sharply, pulling out into the fast lane to overtake a truck that said EQUINE AND BOVINE REMOVALS. PASS WITH CARE.

"Well," said Eva, "there was this poor old widow lady, Mrs Murchison, and she'd got so old that she couldn't look after herself very well. She didn't *want* to leave her house, but the Council decided that she should go into Sheltered Accommodation, where she would be looked after by a warden, and her house, which had got into a very grotty state because it hadn't been repaired, or done over, for years and years, should be pulled down.

"So one department of the Council was to come and fetch the old lady, with her things, in an ambulance, and take her away to the Sheltered Accommodation. And another department, later on, was to come and board up the windows of the house, and nail up the doors, until the demolition people came to knock it down."

"Why couldn't they do that at the same time?"

"That sort of thing always takes a long time to arrange. Don't ask me why."

"So what happened?"

"Oh, do be *quiet*, Eva!"

"What happened," went on Eva, taking no notice of her

husband's protest, "was that the people from the Council got their dates the wrong way round. The boarding-up crew came to the house a month before the ambulance crew. And they didn't hear old Mrs Murchison, who was very weak, letting out a few wails and squeaks from where she lay on the sofa in the back kitchen. They nailed up the door and they boarded up the windows. And it wasn't until the ambulance people came, a month later, that anybody realised anything was wrong."

"Was she dead?" asked one of the children, awestruck.

"Indeed she was. But perhaps," remarked Eva pensively, "she really would have preferred it that way. Perhaps she'd rather die in her own home—even if it was a bit dark and stuffy, with no view out of the windows—perhaps she'd prefer that to being wheeled off against her will in an ambulance."

"I wouldn't," said one of the girls.

"Be quiet, Lecky! How can you tell what you'd like?"

"If it was me, I'd sooner swallow some pills."

"Ah, but perhaps you wouldn't have the pills to swallow. How can you tell she had?"

"Perhaps she was too weak to walk as far as the bathroom."

Trying to ignore the chatter, Ewart plunged back into the past.

The river had been brown, the colour of amber, sliding along over its pebbles. Where it deepened to a ten-foot pool, deep enough to dive into from a rock, there it was darker in colour, like brown ale, or stout, but so clear that you could see right to the bottom, see the sandy bed, and the fish lurking. On the gravel-bed there were quartz stones, purple, white and pink. Up on the moor there were Roman remains to be found, as well as traces of earlier, ancient men, Pictish settlements and stone circles.

They had walked and walked for miles, they had ridden bicycles, they had climbed steep honey-scented rocky hillsides.

What was her name, she, the companion, lost, inaccessible, irrevocably gone?

Was it because of her that all other women, ever since, had seemed so petty, spiteful, dull, antagonistic?

What bliss the return had been, every summer, to find the place unchanging, unchanged. The same in every slightest particular, the little wooden footbridge spanning the brook, the gravel track, the shallow ford. Always they followed the same ritual on arrival, the children would leap from the back seat of the car and ride through the ford standing on the running-board. In those days cars had running-boards. The water would rise in a curved crest on either side but leave them dry. And then, ahead, there lay the cottage, solid, ancient, grey, against its protecting trees and outbuildings. And old Annie to greet them joyfully with their favourite supper. And after supper she would bath them in the oval zinc tub, in the little lean-to washhouse. And during the bathing process she would tell them stories, of Scath the Warrior Queen, of the Ninth Wave, of the Death Weaver at the Pole, or the Three Marvels of Hy. But their favourite of all was the tale of the Bean Nighe, the Washer of the Ford. "Tell about the Bean Nighe, Annie! Please!"

"She stands upon the banks of the stream. The banks have mist and shadow. She has her back turned, always her back turned. And she is washing and slapping at the linen, great ropes of white linen that she lifts from the waters, lifts and drops into the water, lifts again and beats on the stones to cleanse the cloth. And, as the dirt falls from the linen into the waters, so the woman sings and croons: 'O arone, aree, eily arone, arone! O, O, arone, eily arone!' And thus she stands among the shadows as the days come and go, the months come and go, the years come and go."

"But tell what happens, Annie, if she sees you!"

"All is well if you can slip past the woman, slip across the ford as she washes her linen, if you can slip past behind her back without her seeing you, and go on your way. But O, woe, if she should chance to turn and see you, for her face is so terrible that none can bear the sight of it, and she will strike at you in her anger, scream and slap at you with the weight of the heavy wet linen. And then, and then, O woe betide you!"

"What happens, what happens to you, Annie?"

"The Washer will put your death on you, from that day forward your death is upon you, and you will groan with the weight of it. For you will die from hour to hour, and you will die from day to day. Never a moment's peace will you have, from the time when she sets her terrible eyes upon you and strikes at you with the fearsome weight of the wet linen that she holds in her bony hand.

"Now, off with ye, get to bed with ye, the pair of ye."

And she would chase them upstairs to bed, and all night long the voice of the river, its rustle and murmur, would come through the open casement and be in their ears and in their thoughts and lull them into dreams.

"So, what did they do," cried the girls in the back, "what did they do with the old lady in the house, did they bury her?"

"Of course they buried her, stupid, they wanted to pull down the house, didn't they? They took her out and buried her. The Council did that. But there had to be an inquest first."

"Didn't she have any family? Anybody to worry about her?"

"Only a nephew. And he was in New Zealand."

"Oh, do be *quiet.* Or talk about something else," Ewart called to the girls in the back.

"But it's interesting, Daddy. What will they do to you, because of it? Will they send you to prison?"

"Of course they won't do that, children," interposed his smiling wife. "Daddy was only the planning officer, that's not a very important position. But perhaps he will be asked to resign. Or there'll be an inquiry, but they often take a very long time, and don't prove anything."

"What about the man that Daddy ran over? Won't he be sent to prison for that?"

"No, no, the coroner said the man was a risk to the public and to himself."

"So why does his wife want Daddy to pay her all that money?"

"Because thirty years ago he was a well-known singer," said Tish patiently. "Everybody but you knows *that.* He used to make money once, singing his songs, and now his wife won't have that to live on."

"That's not fair. He might just as well have been a street-cleaner."

"Well," said Eva lightly, "it will teach your father to drive more carefully from now on, won't it?"

All of a sudden, Ewart swerved the car on to the hard shoulder and switched off the motor.

"Daddy! What's the matter? What are you doing? Have you run out of petrol? Why are you getting out?"

"What is it, Ewart? Have you got back-ache?"

Eva's voice was mocking, only mildly concerned.

"No. This is where I quit. You can take on the driving. You can take the kids home. There's enough in the tank to get you to Ambley Service Station."

"Ewart! What do you *mean?*"

"Daddy! DADDY!"

But he was already scrambling down the bushy, brambly embankment, he was deaf to the shock and fright in their shrill voices.

She can drive them, he muttered to himself, over and over. She's often told me she's a better driver than I am. Now she can jolly well take over.

There was a high barbed-wire fence at the foot of the bank; he pushed through it, regardless of rips to his jacket and trousers.

And then he was in the woods.

By now it was gathering dusk. Through sloe-bushes and hawthorn, ahead of him, he could see larger trees, and the shape of the round hills, curving on either side. The wooden landscape was silent; perhaps the weather was too cold and too grey for birds to be engaged in their evening chorus. But there was a fresh, wet, cold scent everywhere, a cold northern smell of true country, very different from the stale, used air which hung about the tennis-courts and golf-links of Joplins Super-Holiday Theme Park. He could smell mud, and fungus, and rotten wood, and crushed nettles.

For miles on miles, it seemed, he fought his way through the intractable woodland without ever chancing on a footpath. It seemed as if no human beings ever made use of this land. Deer trails there were, sometimes, or rabbit tracks, but they soon petered out. Yet he struggled on, instinctively keeping a course, walking in a northerly direction. And by degrees the trees, ash and beech, began to give way to smaller ones, alder and wild plum, and these to blackberry clumps; and at last he came out on a grassy hillside, looking down into a valley.

It seemed to him that the contours of this valley were very familiar. By instinct, he turned right, going eastwards, and soon came to a drystone wall, and climbed it. Now, downhill, before him, ran a road, straight as a rule, switchbacking over a series of ridges, making its way directly to the valley bottom. He followed, and he recognised every bush along the way, every clump of broom, every mossy rock on the bank at either side.

If there were voices behind him, at the top of the hill, crying faintly in the twilight wind, he took no notice. Women! he thought, a pack of women, clamouring always at my heels, young and old, clamouring for attention, for money, for things I can't give them, and don't want to give them. The old girl boarded up in the house, the woman whining on about her sot of a husband, Eva, sneering and unsatisfied, the girls yapping after me, day after day, like penny Furies.

I'm happy to be quit of them, and hope I never hear any of their voices, ever again.

At the foot of the hill the way divided, and this, too, he remembered. The tarred road swung right, and a sandy pebbled track led off to the left, downhill, between banks of pale, tussocky grass. This was his way.

Dusk lay about him now, in layers of cold shadow, and it did not seem to him at all strange that, though he had walked for hours now as it seemed, still this same twilight had been about him ever since he left the motorway. It had never grown much darker. It was like the Arctic summer twilight, that lasts all night.

He came to a sharp turn in the lane, and now, ahead, he could hear the twofold music of the brook and the river; the brook a light, bubbling chuckle, near at hand; the river a deeper, louder murmur, the distance of a wide meadow farther on.

He turned a corner of the tussocky bank, and there was the wooden footbridge.

And he saw the shallow ford, and the pebbly slope above it, leading up to the ancient grey cottage, snug among its trees.

And he saw something else.

He saw a woman, clothed in grey, stooping, with her ankles in the shallow water, and a great white mass of woven stuff that she dragged upwards, and shook and pummelled and dropped into the brook again, as if it were a painful, deadly weight to her, and yet she must perform this action, keep performing it, for ever, perhaps. So she stooped, and rose, and worked at her heavy task in the cold gloaming, as if she had been at it since the beginning of the world, through back-breaking ages, and must continue to do it for as many ages to come. And, as she stooped and wrought, and worked and wrung at the linen, she chanted mournful words: "Arone! Aree! O, O, eily arone."

And the shadows gathered round her.

Now it seemed to Ewart that, since she was so deeply engrossed in her strange occupation, and her melancholy song, there might be a chance for him to creep past her across the bridge. For cross it he must, if he were ever to reach the house where he longed to be.

So, with his heart in his mouth, he crept, step by step, towards the water. Now he was perilously close to the strange Washer at her endless task; but still he began to think that he might be able to creep by unseen.

And then, all of a sudden, round she swung, and, O, the look she gave him!

"So it is *you*, is it?" she said, with her terrible eyes on him. "O indeed, and it is a long time I've been waiting for you, Ewart of the pale cheek! Well I remember how in the old days you would pull my hair and pinch my wrist, how you took the ball that was mine, and the arrow that I had made, because it had a better point, how you filled my cup with sand, how it was always you, because you were a boy, that had the better portion of meat or honey-bread, how you pushed my head under in the water and stamped on my toes in the haybarn. O, and indeed you have a score to answer for, Ewart my old playmate, my one-time companion!"

And, lifting the heavy cold mass of her linen out of the brook, she struck him with it, one freezing, stinging blow across the face, which made him reel and gasp and clutch at the air with his hands.

"Mercy! Mercy!" he besought her. "I only wanted—I only wanted—"

But the grey house was fading away into the shadows; fading fast; and now it had vanished entirely.

"What you want," said she, "is not to be had. Is never to be had! And now the doom is on you, and you must go back, step by painful step, the way you came. And you will groan with the weight that is laid upon you. And you will die from day to day."

And that was how it was.

Fastness of Light

"I expect you were pleased to get such a good degree?" one of the women on the interviewing board said kindly.

I muttered an inaudible reply.

"That's hardly the point, is it?" one of the men grunted. "Point is, can she ride a bicycle?"

"Yes I can," I said. Stupid with fright, the last thing I wanted was to have to use my wits, and the thought of riding a bicycle for ever across a flat landscape was infinitely soothing.

The board dismissed me, after firing at me a few questions in French, which I had claimed to be able to speak. In a week or so I learned that I had been granted a position in the filing section of the pensions department of this large government office.

The filing section of the pensions department was housed in a large mansion out in the country, called Holm Hall. It had once been a farm, but in the middle of the nineteenth century had been bought by the retired manufacturer of Judd's Ginger Beer, who remoulded it to his taste, giving it two new wings, a ballroom, a musicians' gallery, and a tower.

Here, fairly soon, I went, to experience a sharper wretchedness than I have ever known at any time since then. It was winter when I arrived at Holm Hall, a particularly bleak, black endless winter. Patches of frozen snow lay in the garden and the ground was baked by cold to a hard, rutted crust. Everything about the house filled me with horror: the impossibly high varnished pine doors and windows, the immense areas of freezing polished floor, the light, shiny, elaborate panelling. It seemed as if no one could ever be at home in such a place —had ever been at home.

I was taken straight away to the clerks' room, brightly lit, full of the smell of red-hot stove. Here sat Miss Vosper, Miss Danby, Miss Craw, Miss Lark, Miss Heatherly, Miss Jones, Miss Bishop, Miss Kidnell. All of them were old, they looked at me gloomily and malevolently, and I could see that they were determined, one and all, to take no sauce from me. Not that I had any intention of proffering sauce; far from it.

Miss Vosper, head of the department, began instructing me in my duties. Twice a day I was to take the mail on my bicycle to the village post office; I was to stick the stamps on the envelopes, and keep a record of letters sent in the post-book. I was shown where the bicycle was kept, and with a sigh of relief I set off carrying the afternoon's batch of out-going letters. The road to the village plunged vertically down from Holm Hall and the brakes on the bicycle were far from efficient; the descent was fraught with anxiety. And on the return journey I wondered if it was worth using a bicycle at all, since it had to be pushed all the way. But at least I could balance the parcels, marked OHMS, on the saddle.

As I walked, pushing the bike, through the large gates, a voice from behind startled me.

"Bang!" it said. "Shot you dead."

I turned round and saw a man grinning at me.

"Know who I am?" he said. "I'm the butler. Everyone calls me Sid. You can too. You're new, aren't you? Come today, didden you? Want to see my blowgun?"

He showed me a little weapon that fired darts, and demon-strated it by shooting a dart at one of the gateposts. It stuck in the wood quivering, and gave me a decided qualm, as I imagined a similar dart quivering in the flesh of my leg.

"I'd better be getting on," I said hurriedly.

"Okeydoke. Tarra, kid. Be seeing you," Sid said, putting another dart in his gun. "I'm after rabbits. The food they give you here is enough to starve a crow. You'll find *that* out soon enough."

When I had finished dealing with the afternoon post Miss Vosper, still with the same air of resigned depression, told me that I had better rule up some cards.

"We keep a record of all the pensions ever paid on these pink cards," she said, showing me a whole room full of index drawers, "but with all these cuts in expenditure the ministry aren't issuing any new ones now, so we use up the backs of the old ones when people have died. Rule the lines *exactly* the same as the printed ones on the front, please."

She established me at a table with a pencil, a ruler, and a three-foot-high stack of pink cards. I settled down to work. It wasn't a bad occupation. The cards were, I suppose, six inches by four, and required to have about ten lines on each, the top two lines somewhat spaced apart, so as to take headings in block letters.

Of course I did not reach my full skill in card-ruling in the first few days; that came only after several months, when I had perfected a system of moving the cards along with my elbow, and could despatch forty a minute, regular as a metronome. The old clerks even unbent to me a little, then, and used to stand round behind me for a few minutes, watching, after the lunch-break.

"Quick, isn't she?" they would say to each other, not entirely approving, but not too disparaging, either.

At the end of my first day's work, when the early winter dusk fell and the shutters were drawn, and I was ready to die from strangeness and home-sickness, we trooped out of the clerks' room and I discovered that I was to share a bedroom with six of them—Miss Veep, Miss Smarte, Miss Robble, Miss Costard, Miss Whettoe, Miss Clewe. They were all in the room when I went in, washing, changing, and grumbling. Whatever I did, humbly unpacking my belongings, arranging my brush and comb, seemed to be followed by a battery of eyes. They said nothing to me.

Downstairs in one of the wide, icy hallways I was pounced on by Sid.

"Come and get warm in my pantry, kiddo," he said, and took me into a bleak hot little room full of oilcloth and tin furniture. There he balanced on the fender and looked at me as if I were a great joke. Sid always wore a waiter's suit, black-and-white, rather soiled. He was balding, hollow-cheeked, handsome in a ravaged, skull-like way, and it didn't take me a moment to fall in love with him. When he began giving me large succulent kisses, though I had never been kissed before in this way and found it remarkable, I nevertheless plunged forward into a new era of experience.

"That's better," said Sid presently, letting go of me and putting us both to rights. "Now you don't look so much like a plucked chicken. Cheez, where do they find 'em?" he said to himself. "Well, reckon I better go and bang the gong. See you some more, kiddo; you and me's going to have fun, I can see that."

He nipped away and banged furiously on a gong the size of King Arthur's round table. As soon as the din began all the lady clerks appeared and glided with decorous frenzy to the dining-room. We sat at long tables. All the clerks had their own little pots and jars of condiment ringed around their places like Stonehenge. I noticed that rabbit was on the menu; Sid's hunting had evidently been successful. Sid and a couple of dour maids served us with silent speed; the lady clerks ate with famished, refined rapacity.

"Please God, don't let me wake up in this place," I prayed that night, and for months of nights after. But nevertheless I continued waking up every day to the same existence of cycling through the snow down the hill, pushing the bike back up again, and ruling lines on the pink cards.

After a month I came down with a terrible cold, and Miss Vosper decreed that I was to sit up in the Tower Room which was less draughty than the little lean-to Post Room where I stuck on the stamps.

The Tower Room occupied the whole top of the tower, and it was filled from side to side with enormously heavy metal filing cabinets, rank behind rank. They stood in grooved runways, and could be shoved sideways, so that access could be obtained to the rear rows. These, of course, held the older and less frequently needed files; if Shakespeare and Chaucer drew pensions, the correspondence about them probably lived here, back in the fourteenth row or thereabouts.

It was warm in the Tower Room, and remarkably quiet; a stray clerk came in very occasionally to put away or take out some ancient letter, but in the main it stayed empty.

Sid popped up sometimes to visit me when I was there; he was not supposed to leave the kitchen quarters but that never worried him.

"Come to the dance tonight, kiddo?" he said one afternoon. "I've got to go into Plymouth after tea. I'll meet you in the village at seven, right?"

I had not even said yes, but of course I would go; I had never been to a dance before, let alone with a butler, but Sid had me under his spell. His cadaverous face, his arms like wishbones, his tremendous fruity kisses like ripe tomatoes were a habit-forming drug.

Seven o'clock found me shivering and sneezing in the porch of the British Legion hut where the dances were held, in my orange dress, with the bicycle propped against the wall round the corner. Groups of sailors and their girls shoved past; Plymouth was only five miles away.

At a quarter to eight I gave up and went home, primly refusing several offers of drinks from complete strangers. My one aim was to get to bed without encountering Sid (who, I presumed, had forgotten all about his invitation) or incurring questions from Miss Veep, Miss Smarte, Miss Robble or the rest of them. In this I was successful, as they were all at the dance.

Next day I felt rather queer and must have looked it, for Miss Vosper gloomily told one of the other clerks to do my post trips, and I was sent to the Tower Room again. I sat ruling lines, with a feeling like crickets chirping inside my head.

Presently, out of the corner of my eye, I noticed something that had never struck me before: there was a crack of light showing between the long filing-cases. I happened to be sitting half turned away from them, and the light in the corner of my eye began to fidget me; had somebody left a light switched on in the very heart of the metal forest? I stood up and pushed two or three cases to one side or the other—but the overhead lights were all switched off, and I sat down again.

After a while, though, I began, as before, to feel a brightness somewhere over to my left, and, turning quickly, I caught a fierce flash of white light among the cases and saw, far down a corridor of stacks, a little man.

He seemed to be signalling to me.

I was greatly startled, for I had not known that any other person was in the room, but I slowly threaded my way to him through the stacks, and found that he had clipped one of the working-boards (we called them pastry-boards) on to a shelf, spread out a lot of papers and geometrical instruments on it, and was very busy, like myself, ruling lines.

"Well me dear," he said, nodding to me in a friendly manner, meanwhile ruling away, much much faster than I could have done. "So you've come up here too, have-ee? Well, make yourself at home, you'm likely to be here a long, long time."

I was feeling strangely drowsy, and leaned against the corner of his shelf, watching the amazing deftness with which he laid dozens of pink cards together and swiftly drew lines across the lot of them.

"You see they meet over there," he said, nodding towards the corner of the room. "Did you know that was infinity, where the lines meet? We're very close to it just here; close —but not quite close enough. It's the speed you work at that makes the difference. I can keep ahead of infinity—if I want to—because I work as fast as light. But I doubt if you can. It's fastness that counts, me dear, fastness every time, in this work."

"But I don't *want* infinity to catch me," I whispered (I was obliged to whisper, because my throat was so sore). "Please tell me how to get away!"

"Well, if you haven't the fastness, you better get inside a circle," he said. "Draw one o' them for yourself—better do it quick. Here's a pair o' compasses."

I took the compasses, fumbling in my haste, and tried to draw a circle, but they slipped and swung and the point stabbed my finger. A tiny bead of blood appeared and, as I stared at it, I suppose infinity caught me.

For a long time I was unconscious, and for a longer time I knew that I was in bed somewhere, but thought, just the same, that I was a captive balloon held on the end of a string by the small man, who, from time to time, gave my string a tweak just to remind me that I now belonged to him. The light round him was unbearably bright and white, and the only way to avoid him was to keep my eyes shut.

After hundreds of hours I opened them and found Sid bringing me a cup of beef tea. He gave me a casual kiss and a grin.

"Hiya, Sleeping Beauty," he said. "Thought you were a goner, we all did. Gave us all a scare, you did."

"What happened to me?"

"Pewmonia, that's all. Here, swaller this and go to by-byes again."

When I was recovered and once more sitting up in the Tower Room I found that spring had come. The darkness that descended like a shutter from tea-time to breakfast had lifted; in its place long light evenings drifted by; cuckoos called.

A new girl had come to do the post, because I had been promoted. The new girl's name was Maize, and she was covered with freckles, had hair like black silk dipped in copper, and eyes bright as blue coals.

Maize feared nothing and nobody; when Miss Vosper treated her to a withering, gloomy disparaging glare she said loudly, "Yer slip's showing, ducks!" She addressed all the aged clerks by their first names and never even noticed their outrage; but she referred to them as old cats when she was with me and wondered how I had stood them for so long.

Maize could not stick Holm Hall. She wept furious raging tears as she tried to add the post-book—her addition always came out wrong. The cards she ruled (about three to the hour) were dirty, crooked, and blotted with misery and fury. She constantly threatened to run away 'ome, and only occasionally cheered up when taking long evening cycle rides with me. We used to drink cider at a couple of pubs and then whizz down the vertical hills with no brakes, shrieking and cheering each other on.

Speed had a fascination for me at this time; I knew, or thought I knew, that my vision of the old man in the Tower Room had been only a delirious dream, but nevertheless the thought of infinity just around the corner persisted, and I was resolved to keep ahead of it if I could.

The azaleas in the untended garden came out and garlanded Holm Hall with their fierce sweet scent. It became very hot. The Tower Room was hardly tolerable now, but I still went there to do my work because of the peace and seclusion and the huge view from its windows down the summer valley.

One day when I was up there ruling away, quick as lightning, I saw, far down among the stacks, the same silvery gleam that I had seen before.

Oh no, I thought in a panic, not again, not now! and I was making for the door when I heard voices on the stairs.

It was Sid and Maize.

"Is she here?" Sid said. He glanced round the corner but missed me, standing among the stacks. He had not been up here to see me for a long time.

"No—nobody ain't here," said Maize, and then I saw them move together as if they had been waiting for this moment all their lives; Sid's hands dug deep into her old blue cotton dress; the pair of them fitted like a jigsaw puzzle: in, out, in, out. They stood, a breathing statue, by my empty chair and the scattered pink cards on the pastry-board.

Choking, betrayed, I turned and burrowed among the shelves, for there was no other way out, save past that intense silence.

Light beckoned me, and I made for it.

"Ah," said the old man. "It's you again, is it? In trouble again, are you? Didden you get inside that circle, like I told you?"

"A circle's no use!" I gasped. "Help me, please help me!"

"Now, now," he said, "take it easy. You can't go as fast as all that, not in a panic like you are. That's the wrong kind o' fastness entirely. Look here, now—" He handed me a mirror. "Take a look into that, now."

I gazed, and could not stop gazing. For there was my face, sure enough; but where the eyes should have been I saw nothing but two shining holes, and when I looked through those, it seemed to me that I could see farther and farther in, to an infinite distance.

"Take it easy," the old man said again. "You can see there's naught to worry about."

I was uncertain how to accept this news of the shining, empty universe inside me. I would rather have laid my head down on Sid's shoulder and wept; but that was out of the question; he and Maize had left by the time I came out from among the stacks; and that evening they went off to Liverpool together.

I have never been able to catch up with the old man since that day, but during the course of my long and peaceful life I have often remembered him with gratitude.